HOUND AT THE HOSPITAL

'I don't know what Danny and Wendy will do if Sasha doesn't make it,' the vet said. 'They both adore that dog.'

Me too, Mandy thought.

A full hour went by. Rupert, the sweet little mongrel, had come round fully from his anaesthetic and his prospects looked good. But what about poor Sasha? The brave hound had risked her own life to save an unknown, terrified stranger.

The hand on the clock ticked forward. Would she make it? Or would she die on the operating table?

Animal Ark series

LUCY DANIELS

Hound

— *at the* —

Hospital

Illustrations by Jenny Gregory

**Hodder
Children's
Books**

a division of Hodder Headline plc

Special thanks to Jenny Oldfield,
Thanks also to Terence Bate, BVSc, LLB, MRCVS, retired Chief
Veterinary Officer for the RSPCA, for checking the veterinary
information contained in this book.

First published in Great Britain in 1998
by Hodder Children's Books

A Catalogue record for this book is available from the British Library

ISBN 0 340 69956 6

Typeset by Avon Dataset Ltd, Bidford-on-Avon, Warks

Printed and bound in Great Britain by
Clays Ltd, St Ives plc

Hodder Children's Books
a division of Hodder Headline plc
338 Euston Road
London NW1 3BH

One

'Today's the day!' Mandy Hope announced when she came down to breakfast.

She gazed out of the kitchen window at the sunny skies, the rolling green hills and the steep sweep of Walton Moor.

'How come?' Munching toast and marmalade, her father, Adam Hope, peered over her shoulder. 'It looks the same as any other day to me.'

It was another working day at Animal Ark, where Adam and Emily Hope ran their busy veterinary practice from home in the small Yorkshire village of Welford. In less than an hour there would be a row of cars and Land-rovers parked in the small carpark outside the surgery, a modern extension at the back of the house. The waiting-room would be crowded with cats suffering from cut paws and furballs, lame dogs, and owners who were worried that their pet rabbits weren't eating properly.

'You know!' Mandy insisted. She grabbed her schoolbag from the kitchen table, ready to cycle to Welford village green where she was to meet her friend, James Hunter. 'It's Monday, remember!'

'Monday . . . ?' Adam Hope brushed breakfast crumbs from his T-shirt on to the back doorstep. 'Let's see. Today I have to vaccinate Toby and Pandora against kennel cough. Then I have to call in at High Cross to take a look at a couple of Lydia Fawcett's goat kids . . .'

'Da-ad!' Mandy protested. She ducked past him and grabbed her bike, which was propped against the side of the house. As she sat astride, flicking her blonde hair back from her face, she felt a thrill of excitement. 'Think about it. Where's Mum right now?'

'Um-mm. On her way to Walton.'

'Right. And what for?'

'Let's see. To meet Danny Davies.' Adam

Hope's eyes twinkled and he gave Mandy a lopsided grin.

The Hopes had known Danny Davies for years. He worked in London as an inspector for the RSPCA and was visiting Yorkshire as part of a nationwide tour of schools. The plan was for Emily Hope to meet him at Walton and guide his car to Mandy's own school, Walton Moor, where she had arranged for him to give a talk later that morning.

Mandy raised her eyebrows at her dad. Her own blue eyes sparkled. 'And who else is Mum meeting?'

This was it. The thing that was to make a Monday at the end of the summer term so special.

Adam Hope's grin spread across his bearded face. 'You must be talking about Sasha!'

Mandy nodded and set off, the wind in her hair, the sun on her face. She waved goodbye to her dad at the gate and rode on, eager to get to school early.

'Hi!' She greeted James a few minutes later by the green, hardly bothering to slow down as she passed. 'Let's try and get there before Danny and Sasha arrive!'

James gave a puzzled frown and cycled hard

to catch Mandy up. 'I take it you mean Danny Davies?' He'd heard about the inspector's planned talk. 'But who's Sasha?'

'Who's Sasha?' Mandy echoed, glancing over her shoulder, then pedalling hard. 'I'll give you some clues: Sasha is eight years old. She's tan and black and white.'

'With four legs and a tail?' It all began to make sense to James. There was an animal involved in Mandy's mad dash to get to school early.

'Yep. And floppy ears and a black, snuffly nose.' Mandy cycled hard up the steep hill on to Walton Moor. 'Sasha's a beagle, which is a member of the hound group,' she told James. 'I've seen a photo of her, and I have to say she has the most beautiful big brown eyes in the entire world!'

Sasha sat quietly in front of the school audience. Her ears flopped forwards, her broad pink tongue lolled.

From her place near the front, Mandy could just about make out the colours on the beagle's short, dense coat. Sasha's chest, legs and muzzle were white, as was the tip of her strong, straight tail. Her head and ears were tan, and a saddle of black fur marked her back. Sitting with her

stocky back legs curled under her, and resting her weight on her straight forelegs, the dog looked alert and curious.

'... The RSPCA has two animal hospitals in London, one in Birmingham and one in Manchester.' Danny, a tall thin man with a wide smile, stood to explain the society's work with the aid of a video. He wore a pale blue shirt with dark blue epaulettes, part of his RSPCA uniform. Pictures of the London hospital where he worked came up on screen.

For a couple of seconds Mandy tore her gaze away from the adorable Sasha and glanced at the film. She caught sight of her mum sitting quietly to one side of the inspector, with the biology teacher, Miss Temple, at his other side. Emily Hope smiled at Mandy, the corners of her mouth twitching in her freckled face. She saw that Mandy was finding it hard to concentrate on anything except the real, live dog.

Danny pressed the pause button. 'Here in the north of England, we have a wildlife hospital, and we run clinics in many of our city branches. We will help any animal in an emergency. But then we talk to each owner, and if they can afford to pay for their pet's future treatment, we refer them to a good private veterinary practice – like Animal Ark,' Danny explained. He turned and smiled at Emily Hope. 'Otherwise, we depend on donations from the public in order to run our service, and to pay for the treatment of pets whose owners can't afford it.' He pressed 'Play' and the video showed scenes of a crowded waiting-room. 'In other words, the RSPCA relies on the money you give.'

Sasha cocked her head to one side, letting one ear flop over her eye. She stood up and eased her back legs, padding across the front of the school hall on her heavy, round feet. Mandy followed every movement.

'So, if an animal is run over and brought into hospital, we X-ray, and, if necessary, operate to save its life. If a stray dog is found roaming the streets, my job is to bring it in. If it has no collar or name-tag, we set about finding a new owner for it. We also neuter animals when owners can't afford to pay for their pet to be neutered at a private practice, because unwanted kittens and puppies are a major problem in our cities.'

Danny let the video play on, showing examples of the pets rescued and rehomed by the RSPCA, and went to sit down between Emily Hope and Miss Temple.

As Sasha wagged her tail and trotted back to settle at Danny's feet, Mandy turned to the screen. She saw the spotless stainless-steel cages of the RSPCA catteries, the shiny white tiles and the bright lights of the operating theatres. There were shelves lined with instruments and dressings, tubes and plastic trays and rooms equipped with metal stands and complicated X-ray machinery. The staff of the hospital wore green surgical gowns and white clogs, or white nurses' uniforms, as they bustled along the clean corridors.

Mandy stared, fascinated. *What a wonderful place to work!*

'It's not that I don't love Welford and all the animals here,' Mandy told Danny Davies later that day. She was confessing how curious she felt about life in a big animal hospital.

The inspector had come back to Animal Ark to have tea with the Hopes after a day of visiting schools in the area. They sat in the garden sipping cold drinks in the long evening shadows.

'Even Mrs Ponsonby's spoilt Pekinese is quite lovable really – though possibly not as perfect as Sasha!' Kneeling on the grass, Mandy grinned and put her arm around the hound's shoulder.

'You hear that, Sasha?' Danny laughed. 'You've got a fan in Mandy.'

The dog twitched her floppy ears and wagged her tail.

Mandy blushed and went on. 'It's just that working in that big animal hospital we saw on the video looked really exciting!'

Danny glanced at Emily Hope. 'We get our fair share of de-fleaing cats, and dogs with cut paw pads in London,' he warned Mandy. 'The video tends to show you the more interesting bits.'

'Yes, and we get more large animal work than the vets in cities,' Adam Hope put in. 'I don't suppose Danny sees too many cows and horses in the course of a normal day's work.'

'Chihuahuas with infected anal glands, yes!' Danny grinned. 'Cows with mastitis or milk fever, no! But although we don't see many cows and other farm animals, the RSPCA hospitals do see an amazingly large variety of wildlife. People often forget that there are some large parks and other open spaces in cities, and they all contain lots of wild animals and birds.'

Emily Hope got up from her cane chair and straightened her cream linen shorts and white T-shirt. She slipped her bare feet into her sandals to go into the house and fetch sandwiches for tea. 'I know what you mean, Mandy,' she said thoughtfully. 'When I was watching the video this morning, it reminded me of my early days as a vet in Sheffield. There's always a buzz about city life, and that spills over into the work you do with animals there.'

Mandy looked up at her and nodded eagerly. 'Did you see that poor lurcher with scabies?' She reminded her mum about the pathetic dog on the video who had been brought into the hospital with hardly a hair left on her body, covered in scaly, itching skin and cruel sores. 'And the ginger cat who'd been abandoned in the empty flat? And then there was the pit bull terrier that was used for dog-fighting!' The commentary had told them that the three incidents had all happened within one busy but typical day.

'Give me a good-natured cow with ringworm any day!' Adam Hope sighed from the depths of his cushioned lounger.

As Emily Hope disappeared into the house, her red hair scrunched into a casual ponytail, Danny looked thoughtfully at Mandy. 'Your mum tells me you want to follow in the family footsteps and become a vet when you're older.'

Mandy felt Sasha nestle more closely towards her. The affectionate dog's tail thumped gently against her side. 'More than anything!' she murmured.

Danny sniffed and gave a short nod. 'And you help here at Animal Ark during weekends and holidays?'

'Try and stop her!' Adam Hope interrupted with a grin. 'Mandy eats, sleeps and dreams

animals! You should see her bedroom walls.
They're covered in posters of ponies, donkeys,
puppies, kittens . . . !'

'So how would it be if she broadened her
experience?' Danny asked, testing the ground
with Mandy's dad before he asked her directly.

Broadened . . . my . . . experience? Mandy puzzled
over the phrase while the grown-ups talked. She
stroked Sasha's velvety ears and scratched her
long muzzle.

'I could collect her from here at the end of
the week, when I've finished my school tour,'
Danny was explaining. 'That is, if you don't have
anything else planned for Mandy at the
beginning of the school holiday.'

'Nothing at the moment. Of course, we'd
need to have a word with Emily about it. But I
can't see any reason why not,' Adam said, sitting
up straight in his chair and nodding slowly.

Mandy frowned. Did Danny mean what she
thought he meant? She felt her heartbeat
quicken and she got to her feet as she saw her
mum coming back with a tray of food.

Sasha sprang up too and trotted eagerly
towards Emily Hope. She barked once: a short,
sharp, excited sound.

'What is it?' Mandy's mum answered

pleasantly. 'If it's food you want, these sandwiches aren't for you!'

'Never mind the food for a moment,' Adam Hope cut in. He took the tray from his wife. 'Danny's just made Mandy an offer!'

'What offer?' Mandy turned from one to the other. She thought she understood what was going on, but the idea was too amazing to take in at first.

The RSPCA inspector got to his feet and cleared his throat for a formal invitation. He turned to Emily to put it to her first, as Adam had suggested. 'I was wondering if Mandy would like to come to London with me to spend a few days at the animal hospital.'

Mandy gasped. She saw her mum's face break into a smile.

'What a good idea,' Emily Hope said.

Danny turned back to Mandy. 'How about it? Bring a friend to keep you company, if you like. You could stay for a week or so, and help in the hospital.' He paused, smiling at Mandy's wide-open mouth and surprised blue eyes. 'How does that sound?' he repeated.

Sasha wagged her tail and barked.

Mandy looked at the beagle and beamed. 'Wonderful!' she replied.

Two

It had to be James who came with her. He was as animal-mad as Mandy herself.

'Would I like to go to the animal hospital for a week?' He'd echoed her words when she'd cycled to his house to ask him that evening. 'Would I like to stay in London and work with the RSPCA inspector?'

'Well?' Mandy had bitten her lip to stop herself from grinning too broadly. Inside, she was bubbling over with excitement.

James had stood on the doorstep and looked doubtful at first. 'Well, I don't know . . .'

Her face had fallen. 'Do you mean you don't want to come?'

'I'm joking!' A flushed look had spread across his face. 'Joke, Mandy... OK? Look, the answer's "yes", a big fat "yes"!'

James's mum and dad had talked with the Hopes and then agreed that it was an opportunity not to be missed.

'You know what one of the best things is?' Mandy had said to him over and over during the seemingly endless week of waiting.

'Getting to drive round London in the official RSPCA van?' James had mentioned one of the treats he was most looking forward to.

'There's that,' Mandy had admitted. 'But no, something else.'

'Doing a night shift at the hospital?'

'No, not that either.'

'What then?' James hadn't been able to guess.

'Spending a whole week with Sasha!' Mandy had said at last. For her, the beautiful beagle was a major attraction.

And now here they all were, waving goodbye to Emily and Adam Hope and Mr and Mrs Hunter on the platform of Walton railway station. It was Saturday morning. Mandy and James had dragged themselves through the last

day of term, waiting for the moment when the final bell rang and school broke up for summer.

Danny Davies and Sasha had finished their educational tour on the Thursday, then Danny had returned his hired car and spent Friday resting with the Hopes at Animal Ark.

'Ring us when you arrive!' Mrs Hunter called.

James leaned out of the window of the stationary train. 'Don't worry. We'll be fine.'

''Course they will. Mandy's been to Africa, Australia, America . . .' Mr Hunter confirmed. 'London's only a stone's throw away in comparison.'

Mandy squeezed out of the window beside James. 'Tell Gran and Grandad I hope they have a nice holiday!' she called to her mum and dad. Her grandparents were setting out from Welford in their camper-van on a trip to Scotland. She knew she would miss them all.

'Yes, yes!' Adam Hope knew that Mandy had told them herself at least three times. 'Look after yourselves!'

'And do exactly what Danny tells you!' Emily Hope called, running alongside the train as it began to move out of the station. 'No using your own initiative and going off round the maze of London streets by yourselves!'

Mandy promised and they said goodbye one last time. The platform slipped away, the waving figures grew tiny and disappeared. Mandy, James and Danny sat in their seats by the guard's van. They were London-bound.

'I'll bet you one thing,' Danny challenged. Countryside had given way to town. At Leeds they'd collected Sasha from the guard's van and changed trains on to the fast Intercity network. Already they'd passed through industrial estates, by giant power stations and out-of-town shopping centres.

James had buried his head in a computer magazine, so Mandy was the one who took up the bet. 'What's that?' she muttered. She'd just come back from checking that Sasha was comfortable in her section of the guard's van where dogs were kept during the journey. She read the name of the station they were passing through: Newark. The train gathered speed and clicked smoothly over the steel track.

'I bet you that at the end of one week you'll be longing for some lovely Welford peace and quiet.' Danny had already warned them about the frantic pace of life at the hospital. 'You know, sheep grazing on the rolling green hills, birds soaring over the banks of heather.'

'Never!' Mandy insisted. Surely it would be impossible for her to grow bored with the busy, modern hospital they were to visit?

'How much?' The inspector's face cracked into a wide grin. 'No, I wouldn't be so cruel as to take your money! Just remember what I've said.'

Outside, the blurred landscape grew flatter. Huge fields of wheat flashed by. 'How long have you had Sasha?' Mandy asked Danny, returning to her favourite subject.

'Well, I've had her living with me at home for just under six months,' Danny explained. 'She worked for the police as a sniffer dog.'

'Doing what?' Mandy was curious.

'A variety of things. Beagles are scent hounds, originally used by the kings and queens of England for chasing hares. They can pick up the faintest of scents because of their spectacular sense of smell. It's up to a million times better than a human being's.'

'Wow!' James looked up from his magazine. He liked facts and figures.

'These days they can use beagles to sniff out illegal drugs. That's straightforward police work. Or another example would be if we were on the trail of an illegal dog-fighting or badger-baiting ring. We'd call in the police and use Sasha to lead us to the secret venue and give us the proof we need to bring a case to court.'

'And that was Sasha's job?' Mandy's admiration for the dog grew. She pictured her, nose to the ground, sleuthing along dark streets and alleyways, across inner-city wasteland. Police and the RSPCA inspector would be running to keep up, shining a yellow torch-beam on the heaps of rubble, through cracks in rusty, corrugated-iron sheds. Inside, there would be a huddle of dark, sinister figures, and two pit bull terriers, chained and snarling . . .

'Mandy?' Danny interrupted her daydream. 'I was just telling James that the police retired Sasha from active service at the beginning of the year. The plan was to rehome her in the normal way by finding a suitable new owner who was prepared to take on a still very energetic and active dog. But the truth is, Sasha and I had worked together on dozens of cases, and I couldn't bear to see her go to strangers.'

'So you adopted her?' Mandy leaned her elbows on the table and smiled at Danny.

He nodded. 'I talked to my wife, Wendy, and we broke the rule of a lifetime.'

'How come?' James's glasses flashed in a reflection of the hot sun's rays. He pushed his fringe back from his forehead and took a swig from a can of cool lemonade.

'In my job, I come across literally hundreds of dogs and cats whom I'd love to adopt,' Danny explained. 'Some of these cruelty cases would break your heart if you let them. Anyway, I always promised Wendy that I'd resist the temptation to bring any of them home.'

'Like us at Animal Ark,' Mandy said quietly. 'Mum and Dad say that if we didn't have a rule about not adopting animals, the house would be overrun by them in less than a week!'

'Exactly,' Danny nodded.

'So why was Sasha different?' James wanted to know.

'I'm not sure. I knew there was something special about her from the start. I can't quite put my finger on it.'

'Was it because she's so clever?' James asked.

'Partly.' Danny hesitated.

'And so loyal?' James had noticed how Sasha liked to shadow Danny wherever he went. Even now, they could hear her whining quietly to be let out of the lonely guard's van in the next carriage.

'Partly that, too.'

Mandy got up again and went the few steps down the carriage to the guard's van. Sasha pressed her nose to the wire-mesh kennel door and gazed back mournfully.

In a flash Mandy knew what else it was that had made Danny soften his heart. She stared at Sasha's face, at the drooping ears and soft white cheeks, the square muzzle and broad, black nose, then at the dark brown, pleading gaze. 'It was her eyes,' she murmured. The deep, intense, intelligent look in her eyes.

'What we have here is a typical cat-bite abscess.' House surgeon Barney McGill had invited James and Mandy into his clinic soon after they arrived at the hospital. He showed them a ginger-and-white tom who sat listlessly on the treatment table while his worried owner stood to one side.

'We see a lot of these in spring and summer, when tomcats fight over females,' Barney explained. He parted the thick white fur behind the cat's right ear. 'Often the bite itself isn't serious, but the wound gets infected and forms an abscess.'

'Is it painful?' James asked.

The stocky, middle-aged vet nodded. His white coat hung open over a dark red-and-blue checked shirt. 'Very painful. Mozart here has developed a fever because poison has spread from the abscess into his bloodstream.'

Mandy frowned as Barney turned to the elderly lady owner to ask how long it was since Mozart had stopped eating properly. She could see that the cat was very sick.

'We'll have to fix him up with a drip and keep him in overnight,' the vet decided. 'Fluid from the drip will make up for what Mozart has lost through running a high temperature and not eating or drinking for several days.'

The cat's owner put a wrinkled hand to her mouth and blinked back the tears. 'He will be all right, won't he?'

Barney gave her a reassuring smile. 'We'll start him on a course of antibiotics and we'll dose him with a sedative to help him settle down,' he promised. 'Give us a ring later today and we'll let you know how he is.'

A nurse in a white uniform came in and took Mozart off to the residential unit while his tearful owner left quietly. Barney McGill checked the whiteboard on the wall for his next appointment. 'Monty!' he announced.

James glanced at Mandy as the door swung open and another owner, a boy of about James and Mandy's age, carried a small pet carrier into the room. As far as they were concerned, Monty could have been anything from a hamster to a puppy.

'Meet Monty!' Barney opened the box and lifted the animal out. A small, furry white creature with a brown head and shoulders and a long, thin tail sat in the palm of his hand.

'It's a rat!' James squeaked. Then he blushed and coughed to clear his throat.

'That's right,' said Barney McGill. 'He belongs to a fancy variety called the hooded rat. Don't worry, he's tame.' The vet put Monty gently on the table. 'What seems to be the problem?' he asked the boy.

'He's wheezing a lot.' Monty's owner concentrated on keeping his rat still while the vet examined him. 'He's stopped using his exercise wheel because he gets so out of breath.'

The little rodent squirmed as the vet turned him on to his side and listened to his chest.

'If it was winter, I'd be thinking about bronchitis or pneumonia,' Barney told them. 'Rats get a lot of chest infections in cold weather. But in the summer it's more likely to be some kind of allergy. What bedding do you use in the bottom of Monty's cage?' he asked the boy.

'Sawdust. I change it every day.' He scooped Monty up and held him gently in both hands. The rat's pointed nose and dark, beady eyes peered out from between his fingers.

'Yes. It's important to keep him clean. But I think that Monty may have an allergic reaction to the sawdust. Try using wood shavings instead. It's less dusty and just as comfortable for him.' Barney McGill sounded confident that he'd sorted out the problem.

'Remember, shavings not sawdust in future.' He let the boy put Monty back in his box and watched him carry his pet out of the room.

The busy vet turned to his visitors as he waited for the next patient. 'Good journey?' he asked them.

'Yes, thanks.' Mandy felt that the day had been a blur. She, James, Danny and Sasha had caught the tube from King's Cross station and arrived at the hospital in the early afternoon. Danny had introduced her and James to Barney McGill, left them with him for the afternoon, then gone home to see his wife. Later he would be back with the van to drive James and Mandy round the catchment area he covered.

So far, Barney had shown his excited yet bewildered guests the kennels where the overnight dogs were kept, the intensive care unit for the sickest patients of all, the cattery, and the ward for exotic pets. He'd introduced them to three other vets who worked at the hospital and to half a dozen nurses. After a while, Mandy had given up trying to remember names and had been glad when the introductions stopped and the clinic had begun.

'Tired?' Barney asked now.

'Not too bad,' she lied. The pace had been frantic since the moment they'd arrived. She'd loved every second of it, however.

'Yes, exhausted!' James confessed.

Barney quickly checked the list on the wall. 'Well, listen, I've only got a couple of routine jabs left to give. The clinic's winding down for the afternoon. Why don't you two go to the staffroom for a cold drink and a biscuit?'

They agreed, and were following Barney's directions down the corridor when one of the nurses burst through another door, followed by another young woman in a pale blue uniform-shirt and dark blue trousers. The second woman carried an animal wrapped in a green sheet.

Only its black head was visible, lolling from the sheet, eyes closed.

'Suspected pyo!' the nurse warned. 'The patient is unconscious. Emergency admission!'

Mandy and James stopped in their tracks as the nurse and the ambulance driver rushed by.

'Pyometra,' Barney told them as he came out of the treatment room and led the way to another, larger room that led into an operating theatre beyond. 'Want to watch?'

'What is it?' James had never heard the word.

But Mandy nodded and followed. She knew it from the surgery at home. Pyometra was common and easily recognised. It was when a bitch's womb became infected. The poor thing had probably been refusing to eat, drinking a lot and vomiting it all up. 'Are you going to operate?'

Barney said that he probably would. 'But not right now. First we'll fix her up with a drip and do some blood tests to check liver and kidney functions.'

James went slowly after the others into the prep room. He saw the nurse take the sheet away from the unconscious dog after the ambulance driver had laid her on the table. She was a black-and-white Border collie, lying on her side, legs stretched straight out.

'Her name's Poppy,' the ambulance driver reported. 'She's ten years old. The owner's in reception. He was too upset to come through.'

'It looks as if she could have kidney failure. Let's get some fluid into her.' Barney's pleasant, unruffled face looked suddenly serious. He wheeled a metal stand into place, attached a long catheter tube to a plastic pack of fluid, then prepared a syringe.

Meanwhile, the nurse took an electric razor and shaved a patch of fur from Poppy's foreleg.

James grimaced at the sight of the needle. He turned his head and stared at the wall.

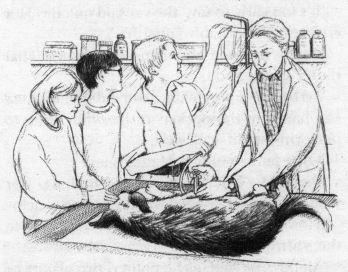

But Mandy wasn't squeamish. She watched anxiously as the vet inserted the needle into a vein, then attached the catheter. The nurse strapped it firmly into place. Within seconds, the drip was in place and working.

'OK, let's monitor her for twenty-four hours,' Barney decided. He ordered blood tests, then asked the nurse to wheel Poppy on to the ward. As the prep room emptied, he took a deep breath and turned again to Mandy and James.

'Will she be OK?' Mandy watched the patient disappear along the corridor. She found that tension had made her dig her fingernails into the palms of her hands.

'It's too early to say,' the vet said quietly. 'Her chances are probably fifty-fifty.'

Mandy frowned and glanced at James. That didn't sound good.

'I'd better go and tell her owner.' The vet went off, hands in the pockets of his white coat, to perform the difficult task.

'OK?' James studied Mandy's face.

She gave a brief nod, but said nothing. Her mouth felt dry, her head was beginning to ache.

'How about that drink?' He led the way to the staffroom.

'Mandy,' he said, as he poured two glasses of

juice. 'Remember Danny's bet about us missing Welford?'

She sank into a chair, almost swamped by the pace of hospital life. 'So?'

James looked at her long and hard. 'What if he was right?' he murmured awkwardly. 'What if we aren't cut out for this after all?'

Three

It was the end of Mandy and James's first eventful day at the animal hospital; the hot summer sun had cooled and the bustling waiting-room had emptied.

'Mozart's temperature is nearly down to normal,' Barney McGill told them as they sat by the open door waiting for Danny and enjoying a breath of fresh air. Outside in the carpark there was an RSPCA ambulance and a short row of cars belonging to the staff. Beyond that, a constant stream of traffic flowed along a dual carriageway leading to one of London's major ring roads.

'Does that mean he'll make it?' Mandy asked. She recalled the ginger-and-white cat's dull, stiff coat and listless, staring eyes.

Barney nodded. 'I'll take him off the drip tomorrow morning, lance the abscess under general anaesthetic, and keep him on the antibiotics for a few days. After that, he should be fine.'

'What about Poppy?' James wanted to know. It had been two hours since the Border collie had been rushed in.

'She's conscious now,' the vet reported. 'The blood tests show a very high white cell count. The white cells are the ones the body produces to fight off infection. But it looks like she's escaped serious liver damage, thank heavens. I've asked the nurses to prepare her for surgery first thing tomorrow morning.'

'Tomorrow's Sunday,' James pointed out without thinking. He was tired from the tense pace of their first day.

Barney smiled and glanced out at a white van that had pulled up outside the door. 'A sick animal doesn't pay any attention to the days of the week,' he reminded James. 'Or to the hour of the day or night. It's twenty-four hours a day, seven days a week here.'

Mandy spotted Danny getting out of the van and letting Sasha out of the passenger door. The beagle trotted gladly up the ramp to greet them, tail carried high and straight, soft ears flapping. Mandy stooped to stroke her. The very sight of the dog's lively face lifted her own flagging spirits.

'Who's ready for a ride around the catchment area?' Danny came up, smart and fresh in his uniform.

'Me!' James jumped up. This had been one of the treats he'd been looking forward to.

'Could you call in on Carl Hickmann at Flat A, 71 Bowling Street?' Barney asked. 'He was supposed to bring his dog in for a check-up today, but he didn't show up.'

Danny nodded and let Mandy and James into the front of the van. Sasha climbed into the back. 'Oh, great!' Mandy said. 'Sasha's coming with us!'

Danny smiled. 'Inspectors don't normally take their own dogs out when they're on duty. But Sasha here, with her police training, is a bit of an exception.' He turned the van out of the carpark, then went on to tell Mandy and James about Rupert, Carl Hickmann's dog.

'He was brought in with a suspected broken

leg a couple of weeks back,' the inspector explained. 'It turned out the leg was only bruised, but Hickmann gave our nurses a rough time. He'd been drinking, and when we said we wanted to keep the dog in overnight, he began to shout and swear. Barney noticed that Rupert seemed terrified.'

Mandy listened carefully. She felt the van swing out on to the dual carriageway and cruise along on the inside lane. 'What happened?' she asked.

'We kept him in and gave him plenty of TLC – tender loving care. Our nurse, Julie, made a big fuss of the little dog. He soon came out of himself; stopped cringing in the corner of his kennel and generally grew much happier.' Danny signalled right at some traffic-lights and waited for them to change to green.

'Then what?' Mandy felt there was no happy ending to this story. She glanced at the rows of small fruit and vegetable shops with outside stalls piled high with bananas, oranges and exotic-looking fresh herbs.

'We suspected that Carl Hickmann was an unsuitable owner, but we had no proof,' Danny went on. 'For a couple of days he didn't even bother to visit Rupert and we began to hope that he'd dumped him. Then we could set about finding the dog a new home. But no such luck. On the third day Hickmann turned up, drunk as usual. Rupert yelped when he saw him and his ears went back.'

'But you had to let him go?' Mandy was shocked.

Danny nodded and set off down a side road. 'We had no choice. The only thing we could do was schedule a follow-up appointment for a check-up. That was today. Since Hickmann didn't show up, it means I can visit the address, remind him about the missed appointment and investigate conditions there. If I find they're unsatisfactory, we might be able to do something about taking the dog away permanently.'

As the van reached the end of a row of tall, terraced houses Mandy noticed a wide expanse of grass and trees behind a set of neat iron railings. Danny pulled up at some gates and said they would let Sasha out for a run in the small park there. 'Open the back door, James,' he said, as he paused to answer his mobile phone.

The beagle leaped from the van and dashed through the park gates. She raced across the breezy open space, barking with joy, pounding over the smooth grass on her well-padded feet. Soon she was sniffing out fascinating scents round the roots of tall trees, following where her nose led her.

'Sasha, come back!' James called. He perched his black baseball cap on the back of his head and set off after her.

The dog ignored him and went from tree to tree. The white tip of her pointed tail bobbed in and out of sight.

Mandy glanced at Danny and saw that he was still speaking on the phone. She too set off across the park. 'Here, girl!' She called the dog back, realising that if they weren't careful, Sasha's curiosity would lead her out through the gates on the other side of the park and on to another road.

But still Sasha followed her nose. She seemed to be getting dangerously close to the stream of fast-moving traffic, rooting in some long grass near the gates opposite.

James broke into a sprint, watched by a couple of girls on rollerblades. Mandy ran after him, saw the wind get under the peak of his cap and lift it clean off his head. The cap flew through the air and went rolling and tumbling across the park. James stopped in surprise and watched it go.

Mandy saw Sasha raise her head from the patch of long grass. The dog saw the cap whipped by the breeze out of James's reach. Quick as a flash, the beagle gave chase. Her sturdy brown, black and white body charged across the park as she bayed and barked after the quarry.

James covered his eyes with his hand. 'Oh no!'

His cap had blown across the grass, through a rose bed, straight into a small paddling-pool.

Sasha charged after it. She grabbed the wet cap and galloped back towards Mandy.

'Good girl!' Mandy seized James's cap and felt Sasha shower her with cold water as she shook herself dry. James joined them while Danny came across the park to discover what the fuss was about.

'She just rescued James's cap!' Mandy praised the clever dog. She grinned at James as he put his soggy cap on.

Danny shook his head and smiled too. Then he looked more serious. 'The phone call was to tell me that a police officer will meet us at Carl Hickmann's place,' he told them.

'What for?' Mention of the police made James

forget his wet cap and pay attention.

'In case we need to force entry into the flat.'
The inspector explained that owners often
refused to let him in if they had something to
hide. The police would be there to back him up
if necessary. 'We hope it won't come to that,
but Barney thought it was best to be on the safe
side.'

Back in the van, Mandy sat quiet and tense.
Now, as they drove on, turning this way and
that through a maze of terraced streets, she felt
that they'd already left the adventure with
James's cap far behind. This was a different,
scarier world, with gangs of kids gathered on
street corners, men drifting in and out of pubs,
young mothers pushing battered pushchairs
along dirty, potholed pavements.

As they turned into Bowling Street, she
shivered slightly in spite of the heat.

Danny leaned out to read the house numbers,
then pulled up in front of number 71.

A woman came out of the tall, terraced house
as Mandy, James and Danny got out of the van.
Danny let Sasha out of the back, then raised his
arm to hail a white police car that cruised down
the street from the opposite direction.

'If it's Carl you want, he's not in,' the woman

warned. She was thin and pale, her mousy hair wispily permed, and straggling over her shoulders.

'How did you know we wanted Carl?' Danny asked, as he ordered Sasha to heel. They noticed two people roar up on a motorbike and stop at a house nearby.

The woman nodded towards the marked RSPCA van. 'Carl's the only one with an animal round here.' Her face was annoyed as she spoke. 'That dog keeps us awake all night, whining and howling the way it does.'

Mandy swallowed back her reply. Dogs only whined and howled if owners were cruel.

'Anyhow, like I say, he's not in,' the woman continued. 'I haven't seen him for at least three days. I've heard his nuisance of a dog, though.' The woman spotted a policewoman getting out of the police car and beat a hasty retreat behind her front door, saying, 'He lives in the basement flat, in case you were wondering.'

They scanned the front of the tall, terraced house.

'Down there!' James pointed to some steps leading down from the main front door. There was a sign at the top saying, 'Flat A'.

Mandy and James started to make their way

down the steps while Danny waited for the police officer. 'Don't do anything until we get there,' he warned. 'It could be dangerous.'

According to the woman, it seemed as if Carl Hickmann had actually abandoned Rupert in the flat. Mandy studied the faded, peeling door of the flat, then bent down to push up the flap of the letterbox. As she leaned slightly against the door, it swung gently open. 'It's not locked!' she whispered in surprise, as Danny, Sasha and the police officer arrived.

At first, all Mandy could make out was a dingy hallway. There were no windows, but dim light filtered through an open doorway from a room at the back of the flat. Soon she was able to see an old black jacket hanging from a hook on the wall, sheets of filthy newspaper lining the floor and an upturned metal water bowl in the far corner. So far there was no sign of Rupert himself.

Danny leaned in through the doorway. 'Mr Hickmann, if you're in there, it's Danny Davies from the RSPCA!'

They stood in the well of the basement steps, waiting for a reply.

'Nothing.' The police officer said, after a while. 'He's gone. And if he's left the door unlocked, it must mean there's nothing in there worth stealing.' She entered the hallway, followed by Danny and Sasha, and put her head around the first door she came to. 'In fact, there's nothing here, full stop!'

Mandy and James went in last. The flat was very smelly, and virtually airless.

'Maybe the woman was wrong,' James whispered. The place gave him the creeps and stopped him from speaking in his normal voice. 'Maybe Carl Hickmann scarpered and took Rupert with him!'

But no. Mandy had a strange feeling that there was something alive in one of these filthy rooms. She saw a door that was shut tight, thought she heard a feeble scratching come from the far side. 'Danny!' she whispered, staring and pointing across the hall.

Sasha had heard the noise too. She was at the door, sniffing and poking her nose against the crack. Then she opened her mouth and gave a sharp bark.

A faint answering bark came back through the door.

'Stand back!' Danny warned again. Sasha backed away and he leaned against the door with his shoulder. Gently he turned the handle.

'It looks like Rupert somehow got himself shut inside here!'

Mandy held her breath. What sort of state would they find the poor dog in? How long had he been in there?

Danny turned the handle and edged the door open a few centimetres. He waited for a few seconds, but still there was silence from inside the room.

'Maybe he's too weak to come out by himself,' Mandy suggested.

'Right, I'm going to open it further,' Danny said.

'Stand clear of the door,' the police officer warned Mandy and James.

Danny pushed it just wide enough to poke his head through the gap.

There was a sudden bark and a rush of cream fur. Sharp teeth snapped as the terrified Rupert charged from his prison.

Sasha sprang back in surprise. The trapped dog saw just enough space to escape. Snarling, he made it through the door. He squeezed between Danny's legs, and along the hall towards the front door.

Mandy stepped across Rupert's path. Too late! He was out of the front door. She turned to run after him. Already Rupert was halfway up the basement steps, heading for the street.

'Mind the traffic!' the policewoman warned, as she and the others followed.

Overhead, cars crawled along the busy street. A motorbike engine roared and set off from the kerb a few houses away.

Mandy was first up the steps after the fleeing dog. But Sasha was quicker. She overtook them on the top step, and saw Rupert run out into the path of the rapidly accelerating motorbike.

'Stop!' Mandy jumped across the pavement and waved at the rider of the bike.

The man in the red helmet and black leather suit roared his engine and rode straight on.

'Rupert, come back!' Mandy cried. She put her hands to her face as the cream-coloured mongrel darted crazily towards the bike. 'No, Sasha!'

To her horror, the beagle was giving chase. In the space of a second, Rupert was throwing himself in the path of the speeding bike and Sasha was hurling herself after him. There was a flash of silver as the shiny bike tilted and caught the sun's rays, a swerve, a screech of brakes, and the yelping of a dog in pain.

Mandy hid her eyes. For what seemed like an

age, as the bike toppled and clattered to the ground, footsteps ran and dogs went on yelping, she didn't dare to take her hands away and look.

Four

'I'm really sorry! I never saw them until it was too late!' The motorcyclist spoke shakily, standing well back from the confused scene before him.

Carl Hickmann's abandoned mongrel lay helpless on the pavement. Sasha lay motionless beside the bike, her collar caught up in the spokes of the front wheel.

'They just came at me,' the man explained to Danny and the police officer. 'The white one didn't look where it was going. It ran straight towards me. The other one looked as if it was trying to cut across its path.'

'Sasha was trying to save Rupert,' James said quietly. He held on to a nearby lamp post to steady himself.

The motorcyclist nodded. 'I swerved as soon as I could. I think I just caught the white one on its back legs. But the bike was out of control by then, sliding out from under me. I hit the second dog full on.' He looked down at Sasha, shaking his head in disbelief.

The policewoman held out both arms to stop curious passers-by from coming in too close.

'How far do you think she was dragged along the road?' Danny asked, as he crouched over the deathly still Sasha.

'A few metres; maybe ten,' the man replied. He was taking it badly. Shock made him drop his helmet as he struggled to unfasten it and take it off.

Mandy reached for the helmet and gave it back. Her own hands shook violently. She saw the back wheel of the bike spin slowly as it lay on the road. What struck her now, after the squealing brakes, the crunching metal and the crying dogs, was the silence.

'Mandy, can you give me a hand?' Danny appealed for help in a calmer voice than she would have expected.

Steeling herself, she went to join him. Sasha lay half-hidden by the crashed machine, eyes closed. 'Is she still alive?'

Danny nodded. 'I think so. We've got to free her from the bike.'

'I'll move it!' the rider volunteered. He made as if to lift the bike by the handlebars.

'No, wait!' Danny said. 'We need to make sure Sasha is disturbed as little as possible.' He supported Sasha's head and neck in his hands, telling Mandy to undo her collar. Having freed Sasha from the spokes of the wheel, Danny then nodded at the man to lift the bike clear.

As Mandy released the collar, she was able to look closely at Sasha's face. There was blood coming from a gash over her eye and a trickle of blood from her mouth.

'Head injuries,' Danny noted. 'But that's not what I'm not concerned about.' He leaned forward to listen to the dog's breathing, then checked her heartbeat by placing his fingertips against the lower part of the chest wall. 'There could be crush injuries, damage to internal organs,' he said hurriedly.

'What now?' Mandy gasped.

Danny looked up. 'James, get some blankets from the van. Put one over Rupert and make sure he stays still. Bring me the others. And bring my first-aid kit with you!'

James ran to the van, his face pale and scared.

'Sasha needs artificial respiration,' Danny told Mandy. 'Her breathing's bad. I think her lungs could have partially collapsed. Have you watched your mum and dad do this?'

Mandy nodded. Gently she drew the dog's head forward and opened her jaws. A few drops of blood dripped on to her hand.

'That's good. Now let's make sure the airway is clear.' Danny put his hand inside Sasha's mouth and pulled her tongue forward. Then he placed two hands over her ribs and pressed gently.

Mandy watched as he released the pressure and waited. One, two, three, four, five seconds; then he pressed again. This time she saw the dog's ribcage lift.

'That's got some air into her lungs,' Danny muttered, waiting five seconds and repeating the action. He looked up at the policewoman, who had been alerting the animal hospital by phone to make things ready for the injured dogs. 'Tell Barney we're on our way!'

By this time, James had placed one blanket over Rupert and brought the first-aid bag to

Danny. Mandy used a second blanket to drape over the lower half of Sasha's body.

'Can you carry on what I'm doing here?' Danny asked, giving way to Mandy, who took over the work on the dog's breathing. Then he took a pad of dressing from his bag and pressed it firmly against the head wound. 'There are no ribs broken,' he told her. 'I'm going to strap the dressing on tight and hope that it stops the bleeding.'

One, two, three, four, five; Mandy pressed down on Sasha's ribs with the heels of her hands.

'Not too hard,' Danny warned. 'You could cause more damage if you use too much force.' He tied the bandage tight around Sasha's head, checked her heartbeat again, then nodded. 'Better!' he murmured.

Telling Mandy to keep going, he turned his attention to Rupert.

'OK, he's in shock and it looks like he's broken one of his back legs.' He explained to James how to roll the mongrel on to the strong canvas sheet he had taken from his bag. 'I'll lift him while you slide the sheet under him as quick as you can.'

James did as he was told. The dog yelped as

they moved him, but lay quiet again as James and Danny took hold of the four corners of the sheet and lifted the patient on the makeshift stretcher. Quickly they carried him to the van and put him into the back. Then they ran back to fetch Sasha.

'Same thing as before,' Danny told James. 'I lift while you slide the sheet underneath.'

They worked fast, easing the sheet under the limp animal.

Mandy's arms ached with the effort of making the dog breathe. She watched the movement of Sasha's ribcage as it rose and fell, listening to her difficult, rasping breaths. But Sasha was still alive. There was a chance that she would make it. With her own heart thumping, Mandy got to her feet and followed the second stretcher to the van.

'OK, take it easy!' the policewoman warned onlookers as they tried to push forward for a closer look.

Mandy and James climbed in the back of the van to be with the patients, while Danny slammed the door and ran to the driver's seat.

'Keep going with the artificial respiration, Mandy!' the inspector said again. For the first time the desperation showed in his breathless, strained voice. 'Once we get to the hospital, Barney will put her on a ventilator to help her breathe. But until then, it's up to you!'

She swallowed hard, felt the van pull out from the kerb. *Two, three, four* . . . she waited for the movement of the ribcage as the bandaged dog struggled to suck air into her lungs. Each second seemed like an age.

James's words from earlier in the day echoed inside her head as Danny sounded his horn and wove his way through the traffic, swinging round corners to avoid jams and find quicker routes. Once more she pressed down on Sasha's ribs, going with the sway of the moving van, praying with every second that they would reach the hospital in time.

'What if we're not cut out for this?' James had said.

Mandy stared at the red patch seeping through the bandage on Sasha's head. She saw that her own hands were stained with blood. 'What if *I'm* not cut out for this?' she asked herself, forcing herself to count, three, four, five, listening with dread to the noisy rasp of air being sucked into Sasha's damaged lungs.

Barney McGill and Julie Ashe, the nurse on

duty, were in the prep room as Mandy and Danny carried Sasha in.

'Go and help James with the other dog,' the vet told Julie.

'Rupert doesn't seem too bad. He should be OK with a shot of painkiller and a drip while you assess Sasha,' Danny said. He and Mandy laid the unconscious dog on the treatment table.

'Oxygen please!' Barney called, the moment he saw Sasha.

The nurse left Rupert with James and ran for the trolley containing the machine that would take over the pumping of oxygen into the beagle's lungs. She wheeled it across to the table, and soon had an oxygen mask strapped round Sasha's muzzle.

The vet nodded and took a quick look at Danny. 'You did well,' he murmured.

'Thank Mandy. She's the one who kept her going on the drive over here.' The inspector allowed himself to slump forward and rest his hands on his knees. The shock of the accident had hit him at last.

Barney nodded. 'Go and phone your wife,' he told Danny gently. 'She'll want to be here.'

So Danny backed out of the prep room,

leaving Sasha in Barney's capable hands.

'Now, painkillers to help stabilise her.' The vet reached for a syringe and gave the injection. 'And a drip, please, Julie.'

Mandy stepped out of the way and joined James at Rupert's side. The injured mongrel was conscious, but his painkiller had already taken effect and he was comfortable. As Julie passed by with the stand for the drip, she whispered a few words of comfort. 'Don't worry about this one. He's going to be fine.'

James took a deep breath and continued to stroke Rupert's head and talk to him softly to reassure him.

Mandy went back to Sasha.

'OK, the oxygen is helping,' Barney reported. He listened to the dog's heartbeat. 'And the drip will bring her out of shock. I need to X-ray her chest before she comes round.'

Once more Julie moved quickly. She and Barney wheeled the whole table with patient and life-saving equipment to the X-ray unit and rolled the overhead machine into position. The vet adjusted the angle and placed a small cassette, containing the X-ray film, under the dog's head. He and Julie backed off, checked that everyone else was safely out of the area and took the photographs. Then the nurse ran to develop the plates.

'Wendy's on her way.' Danny put his head around the prep room door as Barney asked Mandy to help him wheel the patient back. 'How's Sasha doing?'

'Hanging on.' Barney re-checked her oxygen level and began to unwind the blood-soaked bandage from her head.

'What are her chances?' Sasha's owner made it clear that he wanted to be told the truth.

'Difficult to say until I've seen the X-rays.' Barney avoided looking up at Danny as he spoke. 'It depends on what's happened to make her lungs collapse. I don't think it's a broken rib.'

'What else could it be?' Danny insisted.

'Perhaps a diaphragmatic hernia, which is harder to deal with.' The vet was busy transferring the dog on to an anaesthetic machine to keep her deeply unconscious.

'What's that?' James asked Julie, who had come back with the pictures.

She clipped them on to a lighted screen. 'It means there could be a hole in Sasha's diaphragm, which is a kind of muscle between the chest and the abdomen.'

'And what would happen then?' To Mandy this sounded dreadful.

'The dog's organs could get pushed up out of place and into the chest cavity. They could be squeezing Sasha's lungs and making it difficult for her to breathe.' The nurse pointed to shadowy shapes on Sasha's X-rays, waiting for Barney to give his diagnosis.

'Yes,' he decided. 'Unfortunately there's a tear in the diaphragm just there, see?'

Mandy could make out the curved stripes of the ribs on the X-ray, and the line of square, lumpy bones that made up the spine. But she wasn't experienced enough to identify the partially collapsed lungs and the hole in the diaphragm. 'Can you fix it?' she asked anxiously.

Barney asked Julie to wheel the patient into the small operating theatre while he scrubbed his hands at the sink. 'We'll do our best,' he promised. 'I have to get in there, put the organs back in place and sew up the tear. Then we drain the fluid that's gathered around the lungs. After that, they should start to work properly again.'

Shaking water from his hands, the vet advised Danny, Mandy and James to keep an eye on Rupert and wait for Wendy to arrive.

Dazed, Mandy watched the door to the theatre swing open as the beagle was wheeled through, hidden under a sterile sheet, behind a mask, tubes and drips.

'You can't do any more for Sasha right now,' Barney said, before he rushed to begin surgery. 'You've done your bit. Now all you can do is wait.'

Sara Exley, one of Barney's off-duty fellow vets, drove Wendy Davies to the animal hospital. Danny went out to meet them. Through the open door of the prep room, Mandy and James could see the inspector put his arms round his small, dark-haired wife.

Fifteen minutes had gone by. Mandy heard the tick of the clock as the minute hand jerked forward again. The operation continued behind the closed doors of the operating theatre.

Meanwhile, Sara was examining Rupert's injuries.

'See this?' she asked Mandy and James. A slight touch of the mongrel's hip had made him wince in spite of the painkilling injection. 'This is where his problem is.'

'Is it dislocated rather than broken?' Mandy asked.

The young vet nodded. 'It's a typical injury in this kind of road accident. I'll take an X-ray to make sure, then the quicker we can push the joint back into position, the better.'

Sara got to work, giving Rupert a light general anaesthetic to knock him out, and took the photographs. It was James's turn to help, and he hovered anxiously nearby as the vet took and developed the plates.

'Yep,' she said briskly as she clipped them against the screen. 'The left thigh bone, the femur, has been knocked right out of the hip socket by the impact of the bike. How long since the accident happened?' she asked James.

He added it up quickly. 'Just under two hours.'

Sara left the screen and went back to look at the mongrel. 'Luckily he isn't a very big dog, so it shouldn't take too much strength to manipulate the joint. And he can't be more than thirteen or fourteen months old. His joints should be pretty supple.' She stroked the dog's head, then lifted his eyelid to check that he was still unconscious.

'Does that mean you'll be able to push it back into place?' James asked.

'Let's see.' Sara rolled up the sleeves of her white shirt and began to pull and push at the little mongrel's left leg. She eased it and rotated it for a while, listening carefully.

There was a sudden, loud clunk.

'There!' The vet glanced up and smiled. 'It's back. I love that sound!' She told them that Rupert wouldn't need surgery to repair the hip and that he would probably make a complete recovery. But to be on the safe side, she applied a figure-of-eight strapping to prevent the femur from slipping out again while the joint was recovering.

'I wish we could say the same thing about Sasha!' Mandy sighed. The clock showed that the operation had been going on for forty-five minutes. Out in the waiting-room, Danny sat beside his wife, one arm around her shoulder as they both stared miserably at the floor.

'So far so good!' Julie came out of the operating theatre briefly and hurried through the prep room to report to the Davieses on Sasha's progress.

'Fingers crossed,' Sara murmured. She told James and Mandy to watch Rupert as he was coming round. The little dog's tongue slid out of his mouth and licked his top lip as he slowly woke up. 'I don't know what Danny and Wendy will do if Sasha doesn't make it,' Sara continued. 'They both adore that dog.'

Me too, Mandy thought. She realised how much worse the waiting must be for the two owners.

A full hour went by. Rupert had come round fully from his anaesthetic and Sara Exley had taken him off to the recovery ward. His prospects looked good. But what about poor Sasha? The brave dog had risked her own life to save an unknown, terrified stranger.

The hand on the clock ticked forward. Would she make it? Or would she die on the operating table?

Five

After two hours of surgery, Julie Ashe came to speak to Danny and Wendy. Her face looked drained, and her grey eyes and full mouth were serious.

'Barney's just stitching the head wound before we take Sasha up to intensive care,' she told them. 'He'll be out soon to speak to you.'

Wendy gazed blankly at the closed door of the operating theatre. Her straight dark hair fell half over her face as she gripped Danny's hand tight.

Mandy and James could only wait.

At last, Barney McGill appeared at the door.

He pulled his green surgical smock loose at the neck and took a deep breath. Then he walked towards the silent inspector and his wife.

'Sasha made it through the operation,' he told them quietly.

Wendy lowered her head and put a hand over her eyes. Danny held on to her other hand.

'I repaired the tear in her diaphragm and cleaned up the chest cavity,' Barney continued. 'There was quite a lot of internal haemorrhaging, but on the whole the surgery was a success.'

Danny caught the note of caution in the vet's voice. 'So what's the bad news?' he asked.

'Well, the internal bleeding has caused secondary shock. We're finding it hard to bring Sasha round from the anaesthetic and her breathing is very rapid. More than thirty breaths per minute. We've kept her on oxygen for the time being.' Barney clearly found it difficult to give Danny and Wendy the unwelcome news. He sighed and took off his smock, screwing it up and throwing it into a nearby linen bin.

'What about her temperature?' Danny asked.

'Low,' Barney confirmed. 'But we're keeping her body heat up by controlling the temperature in the intensive care unit. Would you like to see her?'

Wendy and Danny nodded and went off with the vet. James and Mandy waited silently, watching through the theatre door as Julie Ashe cleaned down the surfaces and put everything in order.

Sara Exley came into reception and began writing notes in a file. She smiled kindly at Mandy and James. 'Quite a day!'

James nodded. He wanted to know more. 'What'll happen to Sasha now?'

'She'll be kept very quiet in intensive care. She's on a drip, and Barney has used a stimulant drug to help bring her round. She'll get all-night nursing care.'

'And will she be OK?'

'We can't say.' Sara closed the file and took off her glasses, slipping them into the top pocket of her white coat. 'If she gets through the night and copes with the post-operative shock, things will look more promising.'

As James asked questions, Mandy took in the answers as if through a haze. Her mind felt fuzzy and she had to struggle to make sense of the words the young vet was saying.

'Unfortunately, chest and abdomen injuries are the most serious results of an RTA – a road traffic accident. Head injuries may look worse, but we're more likely to be able to fix those.' While Danny and Wendy were out of the room, Sara painted the full gloomy picture. She took off her white coat and loosened her long fair hair from its ponytail before she came to sit beside James and Mandy.

'Are you OK?' Sara asked Mandy. She touched her shoulder and smiled. 'It's always worse when you know the owners and the animal; so much harder to stay cool.'

Mandy nodded. 'Sasha was really brave.'

'She's one of the best,' Sara agreed. 'Listen, I know the plan was for you two to go and stay with Danny and Wendy, but since this has happened, why don't you come and stay with me instead?'

Mandy glanced at James. 'Wouldn't it look rude?'

James shrugged. 'Maybe. But Danny and Wendy might not want to have the bother of looking after us now.'

'For tonight at least,' Sara suggested. 'My flat's just across the road from here.'

Mandy nodded. 'It's probably best.'

'Good. You can ring home from my place to let your parents know what's happening.' Satisfied, Sara went off to tell the others.

When he heard, Danny came down from intensive care. 'You're sure you don't mind?' he checked. There were dark shadows under his eyes, and frown marks between his eyebrows.

Mandy shook her head. 'Of course not. How's Sasha?'

'Conscious. She's just come round from the anaesthetic. She recognised Wendy and gave a little wag of her tail.' Danny managed a faint smile. 'Now, you two go home with Sara. You must both be starving. Sara will look after you and make sure you get something to eat.'

It was all arranged. Mandy and James collected their bags from behind the reception desk.

'Will you ring us if there's any news?' Mandy asked Danny, who was on his way back to join Wendy at Sasha's side.

'Yes.' He turned on the stairs. 'Go home with Sara and try not to worry,' he told them. 'What you need after a day like today is a good night's sleep.'

'And listen, Mandy, if I know you, you're blaming yourself for the accident. But don't!' Emily Hope's calm, warm voice reassured her down the phone.

'I can't help thinking I should have stopped Rupert from running up the steps, then Sasha would never have chased him, and none of this would have happened!' Mandy sat on the sofa in the living-room of Sara Exley's tiny flat, watching James as he made up a bed on the floor with cushions and a sleeping bag.

'There's no point in doing that.' Her mum wanted her to be practical and put what had happened behind her. 'What matters now is for you and James to calm down and get some rest. It's very kind of Sara to put you up at such short notice.'

'What? Oh yes. But, Mum, you should have seen poor Sasha when we brought her in. She'd lost so much blood, and she could hardly breathe!'

'Such a lovely dog too.' Emily Hope paused, then began again. 'Listen, Mandy, if you find the whole thing too upsetting, you don't have to stay for the full week at the hospital. Either your dad or I could drive down early and collect you. Tomorrow's Sunday. That would be a good day for one of us to come.'

For a moment, Mandy was tempted. She thought of her own cosy bedroom at Animal Ark: the animal pictures on the wall; the sunlight on the fields as she looked out of the window. But she resisted. 'No, I'd rather stay here.'

'You don't want to leave Sasha, is that it?'

'Yes.' If she and James stayed as planned, maybe there would be things they could do to help.

'OK. Well, here's your dad. He's overheard what happened and wants to have a word.'

Mandy heard the phone change hands, then her father's voice.

'Hi, love. How are you doing?'

'I'm fine.' Mandy put on a brave voice.

'I take it your first-aid came in handy earlier?'

She told him how she'd taken over from Danny and given Sasha artificial respiration.

Adam Hope listened. 'That's great, love. I'm proud of you.'

'Thanks.' Her eyes filled with tears as she reached out and drew the light white curtain to cut out the gathering dusk. Sara's living-room was bright and cosy with its soft cushions and paper lampshades, and a collection of carved wooden animals on a shelf over the television. But it wasn't home. 'Night, Dad,' she said softly.

'Night, love,' Adam Hope replied, his own voice sounding emotional. 'Sleep well.'

* * *

'Barney's in theatre,' Nurse Julie Ashe reported early next morning, when Sara, James and Mandy arrived at the hospital.

'Not with Sasha again?' Mandy asked anxiously.

For a second, she and James were afraid that the beagle had suffered a relapse.

'No, relax. He's operating on Poppy, the Border collie.' Julie pushed her dark, wavy hair back from her face. She got ready to go with Sara on their morning ward round. 'Who fancies helping to clean the dogs' cages?' she suggested.

'Me!' Mandy and James both volunteered.

'How is Sasha?' Mandy asked, as they followed the nurse and the vet to the main dog ward.

'Holding her own.' Julie entered the ward, where there were about twenty cages of various sizes, each containing a sick dog.

As they went in, Mandy could see that some patients had obvious reasons for being there: broken legs that had been put into plaster splints, or bandaged heads and paws. With other dogs, it was more difficult to tell, though most lay in their cages looking sorry for themselves. There was none of the usual barking and jumping up that Mandy would have expected from fit and healthy dogs.

'Danny and Wendy have been with her since about six o'clock this morning,' Julie told them. 'They didn't go home until after midnight, so they can only have had a few hours' sleep.'

'But, Sara, you said things would be looking better for Sasha if she made it through the night,' Mandy reminded their new friend.

The young vet nodded. 'She's survived the post-operative shock. Her system will still be very weak, though, so we'll have to take one day at a time.' Sara opened the door of a Yorkshire terrier's cage and carefully took the dog's temperature.

'What's wrong with him?' James asked, crouching down to the tiny dog's level.

'Poisoned,' Sara replied briefly. 'Yorkie ate some of his owner's paracetamol tablets, didn't you, boy?'

The little terrier gave a high-pitched yap.

In spite of everything, Mandy and James smiled.

'He looks like he's going to be OK,' Mandy said.

'Yes, because his owner acted quickly and brought him to the hospital as soon as it happened.' Sara went on with her round, while Julie noted down on a chart how much food Yorkie had eaten for breakfast.

'You could take Yorkie for a run in the exercise yard if you like,' Julie told James. 'And do you hear that buzzer?' she said to Mandy. 'That's someone at the front entrance. Would you answer it for us, please? I'll be along in a minute.'

Sunday was a day when there were no clinics at the hospital, though of course there could be emergency admissions on any day of the week. So Mandy ran from the ward and down the corridor, across the reception area, to open the door to a figure in uniform.

It was the policewoman who'd been at 71 Bowling Street with them when the accident had happened. She smiled at Mandy, took off her hat and stepped inside. 'How are the two dogs?' she asked.

As Mandy gave her an update, she led her through to the reception desk. 'What happened to the motorbike rider?' she asked.

'Robbie Jones?' the police officer put her hat on the desk and unbuttoned her jacket. 'He was pretty shocked at first. But of course, we were there as witnesses. And there was no way he was to blame for the accident.'

Mandy agreed. 'I don't think anyone could have avoided it.' In her mind she heard again the screech of tyres as the motorcyclist had wrenched at the brakes and swerved as hard as he could.

'So he won't be charged with any offence,' the policewoman went on. She looked up the stairs towards the intensive care unit to see Danny and Wendy coming down. Both looked pale and strained. Wendy had pushed her hair behind her ears, making her face look thin and pointed. Danny's frown had stayed knotted across his forehead. This time the officer's smile of greeting was full of sympathy.

'Who won't you be charging?' Danny had caught the end of her remark. 'Carl Hickmann?'

'No, I was talking to Mandy about the motorbike rider, Robbie Jones. As a matter of fact, though, it was Hickmann I came to talk to you about.'

'Why? Have you tracked him down?' A small nerve in Danny's jaw throbbed as he spoke through gritted teeth.

'Sorry, no. I took a good look round the flat after you left and he definitely didn't intend anyone to know where he'd gone. Not a single clue; no telephone numbers of flat agencies jotted down, no forwarding address left with the neighbours.'

'You mean he'd cleaned the place out completely?' Danny's frown deepened.

'And left his dog to starve!' Mandy felt a spurt of anger. People like Carl Hickmann deserved to go to prison.

The policewoman nodded. 'We've got plenty of evidence to get him to court and convict him of cruelty and neglect, but not a thing that would help us to find him.' She sighed. 'According to the neighbours, Hickmann was a drifter with a drink problem. No one liked him, so they didn't care when he suddenly disappeared a few days ago.'

'Mandy, Sara thought you might want to help her examine Rupert.' Julie came bustling through from the ward as the inspector and the policewoman talked.

Mandy nodded. After his bad experience with Hickmann, Rupert would need all the love and attention they could give. So she joined Sara Exley just as the vet was lifting the mongrel out of his cage.

'I want to look at his hip,' she explained, putting him on the table.

The little dog shivered and hung his head miserably. Long hair grew above his eyebrows and half-covered his eyes. His black nose quivered.

Mandy stroked him gently while Sara lifted the painful hind leg. The dog yelped but didn't snap or resist.

'There's some swelling around the joint.' Sara explained the reason for his reaction. 'But that'll soon go down.' She too stroked and made a fuss of him. 'On the whole, I'd say you were one lucky little dog!'

Rupert nudged his head against the vet's hand. The tip of his tail wagged faintly.

'He's gorgeous!' Mandy whispered.

'Despite what he's been through,' Sara agreed. 'You'd expect him to hate everything on two legs after what Carl Hickmann did to him. But that's usually the way with mistreated animals. They're very willing to forgive.'

The vet gently lifted Rupert to carry him back to his cage. Then, as James came back with Yorkie from the exercise yard, another visitor appeared at the door to the ward.

At first, Mandy didn't recognise him. The man was about twenty, with short brown hair streaked blond. He wore a leather jacket and seemed nervous.

'I'm Robbie Jones,' he muttered, looking uneasily around the ward of sick animals. He spotted Sara lifting the little mongrel and his frown deepened.

'Right!' James got over his surprise before Mandy. 'You came to see Rupert?'

Robbie nodded shyly. 'How is he?'

'He's going to be fine,' Sara promised. She brought the dog to the bike rider. 'You can stroke him if you like.'

Nervously the man put out his hand. 'I'm not used to dogs.'

'Don't worry, he won't bite.' Sara smiled. 'See, he likes you.'

Rupert nudged Robbie's hand for more affection. Robbie grinned and stroked him. 'At least he doesn't hold the accident against me,' he said with relief.

Mandy smiled at James. They left Robbie Jones with Sara and Rupert, and went to catch up on news from the Davieses. The policewoman had finished talking to them and was on her way out.

'I'm going to drive Wendy home,' Danny told them quietly. 'She needs a break.'

Mandy nodded. 'Would you like us to sit with Sasha while you're away?' she asked.

'Would you?' Wendy Davies considered the offer. She glanced upstairs, half-turning to go back. 'I hate to think of her up there all alone!'

'But *you're* tired, and you're going home,' Danny insisted. He turned to James and Mandy. 'It would be great if you could keep an eye on Sasha but she's still hooked up on to drips and things,' he warned.

'That's OK,' Mandy sounded steadier than she felt.

'She's very weak. She might not recognise you,' Danny added. Then, 'To be honest, we still don't know if she's going to make it.'

'OK.' James put on a determined expression. He went ahead up the stairs.

Mandy followed. She prepared herself for the needles and tubes, the monitor screens and resuscitation equipment. *Sasha will make it*, she told herself, determined to ignore the warning. *James and I will tell her how brave she was and how she has to pull through for Danny and Wendy's sakes!*

INTENSIVE CARE

Six

Still, Mandy wasn't prepared for the actual shock she felt when she followed James into the intensive care unit. Sasha, the sweet-natured beagle hound who had been so full of energy only twenty-four hours earlier, now lay on her side, one ear flopped forward over her bandaged face, gazing blankly at them. The tip of her tail moved a fraction, then stopped.

'The tube looks so horrible,' James whispered.

The dog's suffering was brought home by the fluid drip strapped to her leg. He could hardly bear to look.

'But she's in the best possible place!' Mandy grasped the rim of the unit where Sasha lay to stop her hand from shaking. 'Barney and the rest will look after you here, Sasha,' she said in a low, soothing voice. 'It's a wonderful animal hospital and they're brilliant vets. They know exactly what they're doing!'

The dog's tail moved again; the faintest of wags.

'That's right. You know you can trust them. You've worked with them, you know how much they care.' Mandy didn't care whether Sasha understood the words; the important thing was to show her they were here for her. She drew up a stool and sat close, in a place where the beagle could easily see her. And she began to talk about Danny and Wendy; how their house would seem empty without Sasha, and how Sasha needed to get better for them.

'And *you* want to go home too.' James sat next to Mandy. He blushed, then went on. 'People might think we're nuts talking to you like this,' he confided with an embarrassed grin. 'But we don't care, 'cos we know you understand the important stuff!'

Sasha's gaze followed the sound of James's

voice. Slowly, struggling to focus, she stared at his face.

'You want to get better,' Mandy insisted. 'You want to get strong again. It'll take a few days before you begin to feel OK and you can come out of intensive care. Then the wounds will all heal and you can have your stitches out.'

'And pretty soon you'll be on your feet, and they'll give you great food to build you up. And, listen . . .' James thought of another good point. He went on explaining earnestly to Sasha. 'Mandy and I are only here until the end of this week, and we want to know that you're going to get better and be as good as new before we go back to Welford!'

Mandy nudged him in the side. 'Sasha won't know where Welford is!' she muttered.

James drew back his chin and gave her a quizzical look. 'So? She doesn't know what intensive care is, but it didn't stop you mentioning it!'

Mandy glanced sideways at him. 'You're right!'

He blushed and grinned. 'Are we mad, or what?'

'Mad!' she agreed happily. 'You hear that, Sasha? James and I are crazy!'

As they smiled and talked on, the critically

ill dog raised her head a centimetre and turned it from one to the other. The white tip of her tail moved faintly back and forth. *I'll make it!* she seemed to say. *I won't let you down!*

By Monday morning, Rupert's dislocated hip was so much better that he could begin to put his weight on the leg. Julie Ashe put him on a treatment table and massaged and worked the joint to stop it from stiffening up, while James and Mandy watched her at work.

The abandoned mongrel put up with the treatment without complaining. His cream fringe fell forward over his face, hiding his soft brown eyes; his long, grey-tinged ears flopped down, and his upper lip sprouted a grey-and-white moustache. Though he was a young dog, he had the appearance of a funny old man.

'He's amazing,' Julie told them. 'No sign of meanness in him. Just lots of trust and affection.'

Rupert had turned his head to try to lick her hand. His bushy tail swished from side to side.

'Come and say goodbye to Mozart!' Barney McGill put his head around the door and told James and Mandy that the ginger-and-white cat was about to be discharged. 'Sara lanced the abscess yesterday and the antibiotics have done wonders for him. He's a completely new cat!'

They left Rupert in Julie's capable hands and went next door in time to see Mozart's owner fixing a new red collar around his neck. The old lady's hands shook with excitement.

'There, Mozart, you look very smart!' she said in a pleased, trembly voice. 'I bought it specially for you on my way here. It's got your name and address on, and if I let you wear it, you have to promise me not to get into any more nasty fights!' She wagged a plump finger at him and scolded him gently.

Mandy grinned at James. Here was someone else who talked to animals. She decided she liked Mozart's owner a lot.

'Good luck!' James said to the old lady, going forward to stroke the cat. Mozart sat with his head held high, lapping up the attention.

Then Sara passed by in the corridor, spotted Mandy and James, and paused to ask them if they wanted to check on Poppy with her. 'She's back on the ward,' she told them. 'You can help me take her temperature and check her pulse.'

They followed quickly, relieved to find the Border collie looking alert and bright in an ordinary cage. She stood with her nose to the wire-mesh grille and gave a little bark of pleasure when Sara let Mandy open the door.

'I took her off fluids earlier this morning,' Sara explained as she carried the dog gently to a table. 'We did follow-up blood tests and found the white cell count was already way down, nearly back to normal. There's been no long-term liver or kidney damage.'

'When will she be able to go home?' Mandy asked. She was amazed how much difference a day had made. Twenty-four hours after her operation, Poppy seemed almost completely better.

'Tomorrow, with a bit of luck.' Sara took the dog's temperature and gave a satisfied nod. 'She'll have to come back in ten days' time to have her stitches removed, but apart from that she should be absolutely fine.'

'I wish they all got better as fast as this,' James muttered. Rupert, Mozart and now Poppy; the news so far this morning was all good. But they still hadn't had time to look in on Sasha.

'You mean Sasha?' Quick-thinking Sara picked up on his comment straight away. 'She's improving slowly,' she assured them, looking closely at their anxious faces. 'Go and see if you don't believe me.'

So they sped off along the corridor, upstairs to intensive care, where Wendy Davies was sitting quietly. She turned when she heard the door to the small, well-equipped room open.

'How is she?' Mandy asked.

'Asleep. Her blood pressure's up to normal and they've taken her off the drip,' Wendy reported. 'Her condition is stable.'

'That's brilliant!' James crept forward. 'She looks a whole lot better without the tube.'

'Barney says she has to be kept sedated so she doesn't try to move too much.' Danny's young wife still looked pale and worried. 'She's doing well, but there's a long way to go before we can be sure.'

Mandy looked over James's shoulder at the patient. A nurse had moved Sasha on to her other side, so she faced the opposite way to the day before. 'Is that so she doesn't get bedsores?' Mandy asked.

'Yes. It's just like the people I work with in hospital,' Wendy told her. 'If a dog lies too long in one position, she gets pressure sores.'

'What's your job?' So far, Mandy hadn't had the chance to ask Wendy Davies anything about herself.

'I'm a nurse.' Danny's wife smiled. 'I've taken

a couple of days off work. It's strange; you'd think that I'd be used to traffic accidents and all the terrible injuries, working in a casualty department. But when it happens to someone you love it's still indescribably bad!' She reached into the unit to stroke Sasha. 'Danny's feeling it too.'

'Where is he now?'

'He's on the phone downstairs, trying to rehome a bull terrier that's been brought in.'

'What happened?' James was immediately curious.

'His owners tried to keep him along with another bull terrier and the two were always at each other's throats. The neighbours complained so Danny had to explain to the owners that the breed often fight when they're kept together. Finally he persuaded them to let the Society fetch the younger one in.' Wendy was calm enough today to think about things other than Sasha. 'How are you two getting on at Sara's flat?' she asked.

'Fine!' Mandy replied.

'Great, thanks!' James said he liked the fact that it was so near to the hospital.

'Not too cramped?' Wendy said.

'We like it. It's like camping.' Each night,

Mandy slept on the sofa, and James had his cushions and sleeping bag on the living-room floor.

'Did you know that Danny has picked up a piece of information about Carl Hickmann?' Wendy changed the subject and turned away from Sasha to look at them properly for the first time.

'No!' James looked back eagerly.

'What is it?' Mandy was equally keen.

'I don't know exactly. I gather he's going out to speak to someone. Why don't you find out?'

They nodded, took one more look at the sleeping dog, and moved on. Back downstairs, they found Danny on the phone in reception.

'That was the English Bull Terrier Club,' he told them as he put the phone down. 'They have a list of people who'd like to offer Bandit a home. It shouldn't take us long to select the right one.'

'Bandit's the one who was always getting into fights?' James asked.

Danny nodded. 'His owners kept him and Duke in a tiny yard together. What did they expect?'

'And what's this about a lead on Rupert's owner?' Mandy rushed on. As they stood in the busy reception area, ambulance drivers dashed to and fro with new patients, while people queued outside with their pets, waiting for the doors to the morning clinic to open.

'A *possible* lead,' Danny cautioned them. He reached for his jacket and car keys. 'Want to come?'

No sooner said than they were out of the door at his side, heading for the white van together.

'I had a phone call from a Claire Brown,' Danny explained. 'She lives above the basement flat at 71 Bowling Street. Apparently she has an idea where we might be able to find Carl Hickmann.'

'Didn't we see you on the day of the accident?' Danny asked, as Claire Brown hastily invited them into her ground-floor flat in the large, converted house and motioned for them to sit down.

Mandy also recognised the pale, thin woman with mousy permed hair. She was the one who'd told them that Hickmann lived in the basement flat.

Claire Brown nodded. 'I didn't really want to get involved. It's best not to poke your nose in round here. Especially with the police. When that woman officer started asking questions, I kept my head down.'

'So why have you changed your mind now?' The inspector made himself at home. He sat as if he'd called in for a friendly chat, hitching one foot across his other knee.

'I haven't. Not completely. I still wouldn't want it to get around that I'd talked to you.' She retreated to the window, where she looked out edgily on to the street.

'Fine. This is off the record. I'll make sure your name stays out of it,' Danny reassured her. 'You won't be dragged into any official prosecution unless you want to be.'

'Well, I've had a lot of hassle from Carl Hickmann.' The woman explained why she was talking now. 'Loads of noise and abuse. He was always drunk, see.'

Danny nodded. 'That fits.'

'Well, anyway, he came back.'

'When?' Mandy couldn't stop herself from jumping in.

'Yesterday. Sunday afternoon. Drunk as usual.'

'Was he looking for Rupert?' James asked.

'You've got it.' Claire nodded. 'I heard him going down the steps and swearing. He must have lost his key. Then his girlfriend reminded him that he'd left it unlocked and she opened the door just by giving it a push.'

'Girlfriend?' Danny came in with a quick question.

'Anne-Marie . . . something. I don't know her second name. Anyway, they go inside and see that the dog's gone.'

'How many days had Hickmann stayed away from the flat?' Danny said carefully.

Claire counted on her fingers. 'Wednesday, Thursday . . . five days. Well, he comes banging on my door, asking if I'd seen anything, so I try to tell him about your visit and the accident.'

'How did he react?'

'He hit the roof. More noise, more swearing, as if it's my fault the dog ran out into the road.'

Mandy frowned at James.

'At least she's trying to help,' he whispered.

'I tell him to get lost,' Claire continued. 'If he can't look after his own dog, he deserves whatever he gets.'

'Yes!' James couldn't help himself from agreeing in a loud, determined voice.

Danny raised an eyebrow to keep everyone calm. 'The point is, did he give you any idea where he'd moved on to?'

It was Claire's turn to frown. Her grey eyes half-disappeared behind deep furrows. 'You're joking. He was too drunk to make any sense. And anyway, I'm the last person he'd tell. We didn't get on, remember?'

'So?' The inspector spread the palms of his hands helplessly. Why had Claire Brown dragged them over here?

'Well as far as I knew, he'd split up with this Anne-Marie about two months back, so I was surprised to see her with him yesterday.'

'You think they're back together?'

She nodded. 'It looks like he's moved in with her. He cleared out all his stuff, didn't he?'

'Yes,' James said again. 'The flat's empty.'

'So, I guess he had a problem about moving the dog in with them. When he got it sorted, he came back to collect it. But he was too late.'

'Rupert had gone. *He* was already in hospital with us.' Mandy stressed the word 'he' – Rupert wasn't an *it*!

Danny listened hard. 'And you're telling us that you know where Anne-Marie lives?' he asked.

The suspicious frown stayed fixed on Claire's face as she nodded. 'Sort of.'

'Do you know her address?' Mandy felt that

getting information out of Claire was hard work. But the lead was working out better than any of them had expected.

'Not exactly. I know her sister, Lisa . . . something. I know where *she* lives. It's Flat 28, Fitzroy Court.' Claire turned to Danny. 'Do you know it?'

'Yep.' The inspector stood up with a quick grin. 'That's great, Claire. We owe you one.'

'You won't say it was me who put you on to it?' The frown was still there as she watched Danny, James and Mandy head for the door.

'Not a word,' Danny promised.

'Brilliant!' James said as they drove back through the traffic towards the hospital.

'Something always turns up!' Mandy was feeling good. 'Things usually work out OK in the end!' She was already convinced that they would track down the dreadful Carl Hickmann and bring him to justice.

Danny signalled and pulled out round a parked lorry delivering goods to a shop. 'Don't count your chickens,' he warned. 'We've got to check out the sister's address in Fitzroy Court first. And after that we've got to persuade her to tell us where this Anne-Marie lives!'

'But it's a good start!' Mandy insisted. She wound down the window and rested her elbow on the ledge. Suddenly the busy streets looked colourful and interesting rather than strange and slightly frightening. There were two women in silk saris, their hair hanging down their backs in neat black plaits; a boy rollerblading along the pavement.

They turned off the main road into the hospital carpark.

Mandy and James jumped out of the van as soon as Danny parked. They ran ahead into reception to give Barney, Sara and Julie the good news.

But Barney came out from behind the desk to meet them. His checked shirt was open at the neck, and a stethoscope hung out of his white coat pocket. 'Where's Danny?' he said, his face unsmiling.

'Just coming.' Mandy stopped in her tracks. She could tell straight away that something was wrong. 'Why?'

James grabbed her arm and pointed upstairs to where Wendy stood on the wide top step. Danny's wife was crying.

'No!' Mandy gasped. *Sasha!*

Barney nodded grimly. He looked out

anxiously, waiting for Danny to come through the door. 'Sasha's taken a turn for the worse,' he told him quietly. 'I'm sorry, Danny. Her temperature's gone sky-high and she's lapsing in and out of consciousness.'

'So it's serious.' The inspector said in a faltering voice.

The vet nodded. 'As serious as it gets,' he confirmed, leading Danny up the stairs.

Seven

James and Mandy's feelings seemed to be on a rollercoaster. First they were relieved that Rupert had come through the accident. Then there was the growing hope that Carl Hickmann could be brought to justice. But now their spirits came crashing down. Sasha was very ill again and might die.

All through Monday, as the busy routine at the hospital rushed them from one crisis to another, they knew that the beagle was upstairs fighting for her life.

'This is Dimple.' Barney introduced Mandy to a long-haired white cat while James exercised

Bandit the bull terrier in the back yard.

Mandy had just come down from intensive care. Danny was still sitting upstairs with Wendy, by Sasha's side. 'What happened to her?' she said in a subdued voice. She didn't know if she could get through the day.

'Him,' the vet corrected. He turned the scraggy cat round on the treatment table. Its thick hair was dirty and matted, and there was a runny discharge from its nose. 'He went missing from home about six weeks ago. The owners had given up hope of ever getting him back, but he showed up on the doorstep earlier today.'

'Poor thing. He looks pretty thin.' Mandy watched Barney part Dimple's fur and inspect him for fleas. Underneath the thick coat was a skinny, undernourished cat.

'So would you be if you'd been fending for yourself for weeks on end.' The vet went on examining the patient. He checked his paws and the inside of his mouth and ears. 'He'll need antibiotics for the infection in his nose, and I'm afraid this fur is so badly tangled that we'll have to shave it off.'

'All of it?' Mandy's eyes widened as Dimple gave a thin, pathetic miaow.

Barney nodded. 'Under a general anaesthetic. Julie will use clippers to get rid of it.' He lifted Dimple carefully and placed him in a pet carrier for the nurse to come in and collect.

'How long will the fur take to grow again?' She knew that in one way Dimple had got off lightly and his owners must be relieved to have him back.

'About six months.' Barney buzzed for the nurse. 'But don't worry, Dimple's a tough customer. He must be, to have gone walkabout for that length of time and come back in one piece.'

'Have you got time to do a health check on a tortoise?' Julie asked, as she lifted the carrier. 'His name's Ernie. He's about sixty-five years old. Apparently he's gone off his food and all he wants to do is sleep.'

'Wheel him in,' Barney agreed. Nothing surprised him or caught him off-guard. Once more he invited Mandy to stay and watch.

But Mandy couldn't relax. She shifted restlessly from one foot to the other. 'I thought I might go and check on Sasha again.' In her mind's eye she could still see the thin line on the monitor screen behind the intensive care unit, and hear the faint beep-

beep of the beagle's weakened heartbeat.

Barney shook his head. 'We'll soon hear if there's been any change.'

She sighed then nodded. Julie brought Ernie in. A girl of about six and her mother came in with them. For a while Mandy managed to fix her attention on the tortoise.

Ernie's legs paddled the air as Barney lifted him from his box. His head poked out of his shell on its scrawny leathery neck, and his round eyes blinked in the bright light.

Barney turned him on his back and placed him carefully on the scales. Then he measured him. 'He weighs two kilos and he's 23 centimetres long.'

The nurse noted the information in a file, while the vet opened the tortoise's mouth and examined it. 'There's no mouth rot,' he reported to the mother and daughter.

'So why won't he eat?' The woman wanted to know.

'How old did you say he was?' Barney stood back and had a think. Meanwhile, Ernie crawled slowly across the smooth table.

'Over sixty. He belonged to my grandfather. Then to my father. My father gave him to me when I was twelve. That was sixteen years ago.'

'Hmm. Well, he's a pretty old man, even for a tortoise.' Barney smiled reassuringly. 'He's bound to slow down and take things easy. He'll want to sleep more. And that means he doesn't need to eat as much.'

Mandy watched the little girl stare at the vet with her big blue eyes. She wore her fair hair in a long ponytail. Her face was round and rosy.

'The important thing is to make sure his weight doesn't drop below two kilos during the summer months.'

'Why's that?' The woman was an older version of her daughter; fair and pretty, wearing a white T-shirt and loose, bright blue trousers.

'If he gets any lighter he won't have enough body fat to hibernate through the winter,' Barney explained. 'So give him some treats to tempt him to eat.'

'Such as?' The woman kept her questions short and practical.

'Try him on dandelions. Oh, and strawberries.'

'Strawberries?' The little girl was surprised.

Barney smiled and nodded. 'They love strawberries, believe me!'

So, relieved that nothing was seriously wrong except the slowing down of old age, mother and daughter took Ernie home.

Sasha! Mandy thought again as the room emptied before the next patient came in. The instant there was a lull, her mind flew back to the critically ill beagle. She fidgeted uneasily by the door.

'I know it's hard.' Barney read her mind. 'You're worried about Sasha. But being a vet means keeping your feelings strictly under control. You can't afford to get too involved.'

Mandy nodded. 'I'm trying not to.'

'You're doing very well,' Barney agreed. He glanced at his watch and saw that he had a minute to spare before he was due in the theatre to carry out routine surgery.

For once, and to Mandy's surprise, he dropped his own guard. 'To be honest, operating on Sasha was one of the hardest things I've ever had to do,' he confessed. 'I've known her since she was a puppy, and she's always been one of my favourite animals.'

'I've only known her for a few days. But if I had a dog, I'd want her to be exactly like Sasha,' Mandy whispered.

Barney braced himself for surgery. But, as he walked out of the treatment room, he let Mandy have a further glimpse of how he was feeling.

'Let's face it, if that dog doesn't make it we're all going to feel pretty bad,' he said quietly.

'Still weak, but hanging on,' was the night nurse's report on Sasha early on Tuesday morning.

'The problem is: is she strong enough after her surgery to fight off secondary infections?' Sara explained the crisis to Mandy and James.

They had gathered round the unit as soon as they arrived. Mandy felt downhearted. All through the night she'd kept waking up and hoping that today would see a definite improvement; that they would come in and find the beagle out of danger, even sitting up and looking like her old lively self. A miracle, maybe, but in the middle of the night Mandy couldn't help hoping.

But no; here Sasha was still drifting in and out of consciousness, and now Sara was talking about secondary infections.

'What kind of infections?' James asked, his own face tired after a broken night.

'Pneumonia,' Sara said quietly. 'It was her lungs that had collapsed after the accident, remember. That was because of outside pressure from the other organs. But now the lungs aren't working well because the tiny air sacs inside them are filling up with fluid caused by an infection. That's what pneumonia is. You can actually hear the fluid inside the lungs through the stethoscope. Do you want to listen?' She put her hand in her pocket and offered them the instrument.

Miserably James and Mandy shook their heads.

'We said we'd go with Danny to try to find Carl Hickmann,' James told her.

'Good idea. Danny's in the kennels.' Sara said she'd just seen him there. 'He was taking a visitor to see one of the dogs. I don't know who it was.'

'Mandy, James; you remember Robbie Jones!' Danny greeted them from the yard outside. He and a second man stood watching Rupert move swiftly round the concrete exercise square.

'You're back!' Mandy couldn't hide her surprise.

The shy young motorcyclist stood in the shade of the tall brick wall grinning sheepishly. Today he wasn't wearing his leather jacket, but a black T-shirt with a rock band's logo. He'd had some of the blond streaks cut out of his hair and his face had caught the sun. 'I had to come back to see how the dogs were. See, I can't help feeling it's my fault.'

'You tell him!' Danny insisted. He was forcing himself to be cheerful, putting his own feelings about Sasha to one side. 'I've tried saying it wasn't his fault, but he won't listen to me!'

For a while they stood in silence, watching Rupert hobble up to Robbie. The little mongrel wagged his tail, asking to be stroked.

The tall man bent down and patted him.

'Stick around for a bit,' Danny said to Robbie, backing off towards James and Mandy. 'Make yourself at home.'

'Aren't you staying?' Robbie still looked uneasy. He took his hand away and wiped it on his jeans when Rupert twisted his head and licked it.

Danny shook his head. 'We're trying to find Rupert's owner,' he explained.

'*Ex*-owner!' James pointed out. 'Even if we find him, no way is Rupert going back home with Carl Hickmann.'

'*Ex*-owner. *Ex*-home!' Mandy confirmed. She watched the long-haired cream dog nuzzle against Robbie Jones's legs. Rupert might be homeless, like all the other noisy, abandoned dogs barking from their kennels. But even being homeless was better than the thought of Carl Hickmann 'looking after' him ever again.

'What'll happen to Rupert?' James asked thoughtfully.

Danny had dropped the cheerful front he'd put on for Robbie Jones and was driving silently and glumly towards Fitzroy Court.

'You'll look for a new home for him, won't you?' Mandy couldn't imagine it would be difficult. One look at the little cream face with its bushy eyebrows and untidy grey moustache would win anyone's heart.

'Not us. The hospital doesn't usually rehome animals. We send them out of town to a rehoming centre.'

'When?' James frowned and looked straight ahead. The van had stopped at traffic-lights.

'As soon as Sara and Barney are ready to discharge him.'

'That means more strangers for him to get used to.' James sniffed.

'Afraid so. But that's the system.' As the lights changed to green, Danny turned right and headed for a large block of flats near the dual carriageway.

'How big is the rehoming centre?' Mandy figured it out. If the police, the animal hospital and vets all over London sent strays, abandoned and neglected animals to the out-of-town centre, it must be enormous.

'Pretty big,' Danny admitted. He parked the van in the street next to Fitzroy Court.

'So Rupert will be just one little dog amongst hundreds of others?' Row after row of lonely creatures, each one desperate for a new home. Mandy realised that suddenly his chances didn't seem so good.

Danny locked the van and led them across a forecourt to a lift at the base of the flats. 'That's more or less the picture,' he admitted, pressing a button for the second floor.

'What happens if no one wants him?' James persisted with the uncomfortable questions.

At first the inspector was too busy calling the lift and waiting for people to step out to answer.

Mandy took a sharp breath. She felt the back of her neck prickle, then she stepped forwards, clear of the closing doors. The lift shuddered and began its upward journey.

'If no one comes to the rehoming centre and chooses Rupert, what happens to him?' James repeated.

The lift jerked and stopped at level 2.

'They wait as long as they can,' Danny told him, still concentrating on finding their way to number 28. 'But if they can't find a suitable owner, in the end they have to put the dog to sleep.'

'Lisa?' Danny had pressed the doorbell several times before a woman answered it.

She held the door open a fraction and peered round the edge at Mandy, James and Danny. 'Are you the police?' she asked, studying Danny's uniform.

'No. RSPCA.' The inspector gave her plenty of time to look him up and down. 'Could we come in and have a word with you?'

'What for?'

Through the crack in the door, Mandy could see that the woman was small and dark-haired with light grey eyes. She looked sulky and suspicious.

'If you let us in, we'll be able to explain,' Danny said politely.

'I don't keep animals here.' Lisa kept the door in place. 'Only the ground floor flats are allowed pets.'

'It's not you I want to chat about.' Danny kept

his patience and sounded as casual as he could. 'It's about your sister.'

'Anne-Marie? She's not here.' The sentence came too quick, too forceful.

Mandy glanced sideways at the net-curtained window, along the landing that led to the other flats on the second floor. 'Would you know where she is?' she asked.

Lisa retreated from the narrow gap, ready to close the door. 'Haven't got a clue,' she said shortly.

'Could you tell me where she lives?' Danny had to move quickly if they weren't to go away empty-handed.

'No. She moved out of her old flat last week. I haven't got her new address.' Lisa's voice was bored and weary. She obviously wanted to get rid of them.

The curtain at the window moved slightly. A hand pulled it to one side. Mandy caught sight of a man. He saw her looking in his direction and quickly dropped the curtain back into position.

Danny leaned against the door. 'If you see her, could you ask her to get in touch with me at the animal hospital?' He tried to slip a card with his name and telephone number through the closing gap.

Mandy saw the white card flutter to the floor, then the door clicked shut. She looked once more at the folds of the net curtains, trying to remember the face she'd glimpsed.

'Come on,' Danny sighed, turning away from the blue door. He led James and Mandy towards the lift. 'This is obviously a complete waste of time.'

Eight

'Danny, wait!' Mandy held the door of the lift open.

The inspector peered out from inside the lift. The overhead light drained the colour from his cheeks and made him look tired.

Mandy was sure that what she'd seen was important. 'There was someone else in the flat!'

'While I was talking to Lisa?'

She nodded. 'A man. He must have wanted to see who was at the door. But when he spotted us he stepped back out of sight.'

'Hang on, Mandy. Maybe it was Lisa's boyfriend,' James cautioned. He couldn't see where her thoughts were leading and didn't want her to jump to conclusions. 'In fact, it could've been anybody.'

'Then why didn't he want me to see him?'

'What are you thinking? That it might have been Hickmann?' Danny caught on. 'What did he look like?'

Mandy narrowed her eyes as she recalled the face. 'He was about thirty. Quite stocky, with a double chin. His hair was short and dark. I think he was wearing a blue T-shirt.' She struggled to remember more. 'Oh, and he had a tattoo down one of his arms. His right arm.'

'What kind of tattoo?' James asked.

Mandy faltered. 'I couldn't see that much detail,' she said. 'But it was brightly coloured and stretched almost the length of his forearm.'

Danny nodded and told them both to get into the lift. 'You've given a good description. It'll be useful.'

'Aren't we going to go back?' Reluctantly Mandy stepped inside after James. The doors slid to and the lift went down. What if Carl Hickmann really *was* hiding from them in his girlfriend's sister's flat?

Danny frowned and shook his head. 'There's nothing we can do right now.'

'But we can't let him get away with what he did to Rupert.' By now James was on Mandy's side. 'Shouldn't we do something?'

'What?' Danny waited for the lift doors to open on the ground floor, then strode off towards the parked van. 'If it was Hickmann, he obviously didn't want to talk to us, and that's what you'd expect. And if it really was him, we've achieved the point of the visit, which was to try and find out where he was. So, all in all, it's been a good morning.'

Disappointed, James and Mandy ran after him. Mandy glanced back up at the second floor of Fitzroy Court. The row of brightly coloured doors were shut, the blank windows reflecting the sun.

'What next?' James wanted to know.

Danny sat in the driver's seat and turned the ignition key. 'First we have to find out if the man Mandy saw really is Hickmann. But at the moment I don't quite know how we're going to do that.'

Danny reversed the van out of its parking space. Out on the dual carriageway, a stream of traffic sped by. 'Didn't you see him when he brought Rupert into the hospital that first time?' Mandy asked.

'No. I was off-duty.'

'Did Barney or Sara?'

The inspector shrugged. 'I don't know. But hang on. Sit tight and try not to build up your hopes until we get back and find out who admitted Rupert.' Danny eased his way into the flow of traffic.

Someone must have seen him! Mandy told herself. Cars flashed by in the fast lane. *Someone must know what Carl Hickmann looks like!*

'It was me,' Julie Ashe told Mandy and James. She was in the prep room with Dimple, the white cat who had gone walkabout. The patient was anaesthetised on the table and the nurse was preparing to shave off his matted white fur with some electric clippers. 'I was on duty when Hickmann brought Rupert in.'

Mandy nodded eagerly. 'What do you remember about him?'

Julie turned on the clippers and began work. 'Not much. It was a busy night, I know that. Emergency admissions, call-outs, patients in intensive care. Anyway, I always pay more attention to the animals than their owners.'

'Can't you think of anything?' James asked. 'Was Rupert's owner tall or short? Dark- or fair-haired?'

'Sorry,' Julie's clippers shaved off strips of tangled hair, leaving a clean, short fuzz of white fur beneath. 'All I remember was that he was drunk and shouting his mouth off.'

This wasn't getting them very far, Mandy realised. She watched fascinated as Dimple was transformed by his haircut into a strange, skinny, stick-like creature. 'Did Hickmann have a tattoo?' she said quietly.

Julie glanced up as she turned Dimple on to his other side. 'Now, that *does* ring a bell,' she admitted. 'He did have something tattooed on one of his arms . . . Letters – a name with a pattern surrounding it, I think . . .' The nurse nodded, clippers poised. Her own memory had been jogged by Mandy's question. 'I noticed it when he leaned on the desk to sign the admission form. The name was "Ann" something. "Annabel"? No, "Anne-Marie", maybe.'

'Yes!' James cried. 'Thanks, Julie!'

He and Mandy raced off, leaving a bemused-looking nurse behind them.

'It *was* him!' Mandy rushed ahead of James down the corridor into reception. She spilled out the good news to Danny, who was speaking to a small, middle-aged woman in a white blouse and flower-printed skirt. 'It was Hickmann in Lisa's flat. He gave himself away by his tattoo!'

'Well done.' The inspector smiled briefly. 'But it'll have to wait a while. I'm busy here.'

'Sorry!' Mandy blushed and stepped back.

'No, please!' The grey-haired woman gave way with a smile. 'Go ahead. This tattoo business sounds intriguing.'

So Mandy and James told Danny that Lisa must have been lying all along.

'She said she didn't know her sister's new address,' James reminded him. 'But perhaps Anne-Marie and Hickmann have actually moved in with her!'

'Maybe.' The inspector considered it.

James pressed Danny to know what would happen next. 'When do we go back to Fitzroy Court?' he asked. 'How soon can you arrest Hickmann?'

'That's not how it works.' Danny went through it step by step. 'We don't arrest anyone.'

'No?' Mandy felt a thud of disappointment. She longed to see the cruel owner behind bars.

'No. I notify the police and tell them we have enough grounds for a cruelty case. Then I make out a summons for him to appear in court, which I have to deliver personally.'

'Face to face?' Mandy asked.

Danny nodded.

'How long does it all take?' Another impatient question tumbled out of her mouth.

'It could be weeks before it gets to court.' The inspector saw James's and Mandy's faces fall. 'But don't worry, if I can get the paperwork done, we can go along to the flat tomorrow to serve the summons.'

'Good!' Mandy was glad they would still be here to see that. 'Wednesday!'

'And let's leave it at that for now,' Danny told them. He turned to the visitor. 'Mrs Powers, this is Mandy Hope and James Hunter. James and Mandy, Mrs Powers is chairperson of the English Bull Terrier Club. Could you make yourselves useful and take her along to the kennels to see Bandit, please?'

'Have you come to take Bandit home with you?' Mandy asked the meek-looking Mrs Powers as she and James led her along the corridor.

Mrs Powers touched the bridge of her clear-rimmed glasses and shook her head. 'No. Inspector Davies asked me to come in and check his papers. I have to be sure that Bandit is a pure-bred bull terrier, and ensure that his temperament hasn't been spoiled by ill-treatment.'

'Oh no, it hasn't. I've taken him for exercise in the yard before now and he's soft as anything,' James assured her. He opened the door to the kennels, to a clamour of barks and yelps. 'He just looks fierce, that's all.'

'And he doesn't like other bull terriers,' Mandy chipped in.

'That's normal for the breed. They don't get along well together, I'm afraid.' The lady didn't seem put off by the chorus of barks.

'What happens after you've had a look at him?' Mandy wanted to know.

'If all's well, I choose someone off our adoption list who would be suitable.' Mrs Powers peered through the door at the rows of different-sized kennels. 'Now which one is Bandit?' she asked, ignoring the noise and stepping boldly inside.

Mandy had never seen the bull terrier before. She watched as James went to a kennel and opened the door.

'Meet the mighty Bandit!' he grinned.

Out trundled a rough, tough terrier. His brindle body and white chest were broad and barrel-shaped, his legs were short and stocky. A pair of tiny, slanting eyes were set deep in his enormous, egg-shaped head. He pricked up his small, pointed ears and wagged his thin tail. Then he padded across to James and nuzzled his hand with his black, downturned nose.

'See why he's called Bandit?' James stooped to pat the dog, then grinned up at Mandy.

She stood at a safe distance, noticing the two patches of dark brown hair that surrounded the terrier's eyes. 'He looks as if he's wearing a mask!'

'What do you think of him?' Mrs Powers asked, going forward to stroke him herself. 'Do you think he's an ugly old thing with his sharp teeth and little, piggy eyes?'

'No!' Mandy said without a moment's pause. 'He's great!'

'He is, isn't he?' The club chairperson patted the dog's broad forehead and studied him closely. 'See how his upper teeth close like a vice over his lower set? It's called a scissor bite.'

'And is he a pedigree?' James wanted to know.

'His papers are in order. Did you know that bull terriers were first bred in the eighteenth century as fighting dogs?' Mrs Powers warmed to her subject. 'And there was one famous bull terrier called Pincher in the eighteen-sixties who set a ratting record by killing five hundred rats in thirty-six minutes and twenty-six point five seconds.'

'Phew!' James was impressed.

Bandit looked up at Mrs Powers and gave a deep, gruff bark, as if he was proud of his breeding.

'So what now?' Mandy laughed.

'Now?' Mrs Powers scratched the bony part of the sturdy dog's nose. She chucked him under the chin. 'Now I know precisely the right owners for you, Bandit!' she promised. 'I just need to make a couple of phone calls, and by tomorrow we should have everything arranged!'

'. . . So Dimple the cat has had a skinhead haircut, and Mrs Powers knows just the home for Bandit.' Mandy sat beside Sasha in intensive care, recalling the events of the day. Wendy Davies had taken a break and gone for tea with Barney and Sara in the staffroom, so James and Mandy had taken over. She knew from the slight wag of Sasha's tail that the sound of her voice soothed the sick beagle.

James stood behind the unit, studying Sasha's chart. 'Her temperature's going down,' he said, pointing to the graph. 'That's good, isn't it?'

Mandy nodded. She sounded confident for Sasha's sake. 'It means the antibiotics are zapping the lung infection.'

'And her bandage is off.' James peered over the side of the plastic box.

'Barney took it off earlier today. She looks better without it, doesn't she?' Still weak, still on the fluid drip, but battling on. 'You're a brave girl,' she told her. 'And did I mention that Rupert is being sent off to a rehoming centre as soon as he's better? You remember Rupert? He's the mongrel whose life you saved.'

'Hmm,' James grunted. 'It's a pity there's no such thing as the English Mongrels' Club!'

Mandy glanced up. 'And then there'd be no problem finding him a home,' she agreed. 'There'd be a queue of people lining up to adopt him!'

James sighed. He wandered back to the monitors and avoided Mandy's gaze. 'I just overheard Danny talking on the phone to someone from Alwoodley Rehoming Centre.'

'And?' she prompted. She could tell that James had something important to tell her.

'And they've arranged to come over to collect Rupert,' he confessed.

'When?' Mandy stood up.

James turned towards her. He let his shoulders slump. 'Tomorrow lunchtime.'

'Oh, James, that's terrible!' The Centre would take Rupert and she and James would never see him again. They might never find out what had happened to him.

He nodded and lifted his head. 'It will be if we let it happen,' he agreed.

'What do you mean?' Mandy saw that James's eyes had suddenly got back their spark. He jutted out his chin and strode to the door.

'Well, maybe *we* can find Rupert a home before then!' he said.

The week was flying by. Mandy and James worked at the hospital all day and well into the evening. At night they went home with Sara, had supper and fell into bed.

'Any regrets?' Adam Hope asked Mandy on the phone. It was late on Tuesday night.

'No!' Her answer was quick and sure.

'Still want to be a vet, then?' Her dad sounded amused but satisfied.

'More than ever. But, Dad . . .'

'What, love?' He yawned into the phone.

'I'm missing life at Animal Ark, even though

I love helping out here at the animal hospital.'

'Good for you. I'm glad you can stand the pace.' He'd listened to Mandy's account of the day's events, including their visit with the inspector to Fitzroy Court and James and Mandy's detective work. 'And the noise and the traffic and the pollution!' He reminded her that life in the city wasn't all wonderful.

'I know. I'm looking forward to coming home to Welford for a rest!' she told him.

'"Rest"? What's that?' he joked.

'OK, then. I'll come home to Animal Ark and help you and Mum because you're so old and decrepit!'

Adam Hope laughed. 'What time would you like one of us old fogeys to drive down and pick you up on Friday?' he asked.

'Teatime?' she suggested. Then she added, 'I'm missing you!'

'Likewise. Look after yourself,' he said gently. 'And listen, I'll be agog to hear exactly how James intends to rehome that mongrel!'

Mandy had already told her father about the mystery plan. 'He won't tell me a single thing,' she reminded him. 'He says I have to wait till tomorrow to find out!'

'Well, phone us and let us know.' Mandy's

dad got ready to ring off. 'And go straight to bed, get some sleep.'

'I'll try.' Mandy felt too worked up. A dozen thoughts ran through her head . . . Rupert . . . Alwoodley Rehoming Centre . . . Sasha . . . Wendy and Danny Davies's long vigil . . . Mighty Bandit and meek Mrs Powers. She got changed for bed. The moment her head hit the pillow, she fell asleep.

Nine

'She certainly is a fighter!' Barney McGill listened to Sasha's chest and gave a brief nod.

'Better?' Mandy asked. She hovered by the door of intensive care. Sasha had slept through the night and was now lying awake taking in her surroundings.

The vet nodded again. 'Officially, we'd say her condition is stable, which is something of a miracle, given what she's been through.' He stood up straight and hung his stethoscope round his neck. 'I think it's time to take her off the drip and see if she'll take liquid by mouth.'

'Fantastic!' Mandy felt relief flood through her. It was like coming out of the shadows, looking up and feeling the sun shine on her face.

'Make way for a visitor!' a voice said from behind.

Turning to look down the corridor, Mandy saw Danny and Rupert walking slowly towards her. When he saw her, the little cream dog wagged his tail perkily in spite of his stiff hip.

'Rupert's coming to say goodbye,' Danny told them. 'I've arranged for Maria Froud from Alwoodley to come and collect him at lunch-time. I thought it would cheer Sasha up to see him before he went.'

Mandy waited for Barney to remove the needle from the beagle's leg and clear away the drip. Then she went to stand by Sasha. 'Look who's here!' she murmured.

In came bright little Rupert, bushy tail curved over his back, floppy ears cocked.

Mandy picked him up so that Sasha could see him. 'He wants to say thank you for stopping the motorbike from running right into him and for saving his life!'

Rupert saw Sasha lying still, too weak to sit up. He whined and wriggled in Mandy's arms.

The beagle raised her head. She pushed out her broad pink tongue and licked her top lip. Then slowly she let her head sink on to the blanket.

'That's enough excitement for the moment,' Barney said briskly. He took Rupert from Mandy and told Danny he would take the chance to have a last look at the injured hip before Rupert went away to Alwoodley. He took him down to a treatment room.

'James is downstairs in reception,' Danny told Mandy. 'He said to meet him there. He was looking very secretive. Is he up to something?'

'Yes. But I don't know what.' All morning James had refused to tell. 'Are you coming?' Mandy asked Danny as she backed towards the door.

'No. I'll stay with Sasha for a bit. I'll see you later.' Danny drew up a stool and sat down. 'James says we have to trust him. He's got it all in hand, whatever "it" is!'

'We're going back to Bowling Street!' James announced.

It was ten-thirty on Wednesday morning and he was letting Mandy in on Step One of his plan.

'What for?' Mandy was confused. 'All there is at Bowling Street is Carl Hickmann's empty flat!' Surely James didn't want to have another talk with Claire Brown in the flat above? What would be the point of that?

'Wait and see,' James insisted. 'We're going on the Tube.'

'By ourselves?' Mandy stared at him.

'Yes. I've checked the route with Danny. It's only two stations along on the District line. We

get off on to Bowling Street itself. Danny says
he'll pick us up there at the entrance to the
Tube station in an hour. Then we'll all drive to
Fitzroy Court and try to serve the summons on
Carl Hickmann.'

'B-but . . . !' Mandy followed him slowly to the
main door. She stood to one side as a driver in
his blue uniform rushed past her on an
emergency call-out and climbed into his
ambulance.

'Come on, Mandy!' James stood impatiently
on the ramp, ignoring a cool drizzle. Overhead,
the sky was grey and a breeze was blowing.
'We've got to get a move on.'

'Why? Where are we going exactly?' Still
confused, she gave in and began to run with
him across the carpark. The nearest Tube
station was two hundred metres down the road
from the hospital.

'I told you. Bowling Street.' Looking straight
ahead, letting the drizzle mist up his glasses,
James hugged his secret to him and refused to
say another word.

With her heart in her mouth, Mandy went with
James, following signs to the District line, down
an escalator, along a tiled tunnel. Posters

advertised concerts, books and films. People squeezed on to platforms and crushed into already crowded carriages.

'Nearly there,' James said, after what seemed like only two minutes on the rattling train.

He got up at the next stop and Mandy followed him on to the platform. 'James, what is going on?' she demanded.

'You'll soon see,' he promised.

They half ran along another tunnel, up the escalator this time. Mandy found that they came out on Bowling Street, as James had said, and almost opposite number 71. She sighed and looked at James, who had stopped to glance along the damp street. 'Come on then. It's still raining and I'm getting wet. Since we're here we might as well do whatever it is you want to do.' She crossed the street, checking for traffic. When she reached the far pavement, she noticed that the basement flat had a light on and new blinds at the window.

'Someone's moved in!' Mandy warned James.

'Never mind what's happening at 71A. This is a long shot,' he muttered, looking at each car parked by the side of the road as he marched on up the street, 'but it's the best chance Rupert's got!'

'James!' Mandy pleaded. She ran to keep up. They passed house numbers 75 and 77. 'What on earth is going on?'

He ignored her and finally stopped outside number 83. 'There!' James stood with his hands in his pockets, staring at a shiny red motorbike that was parked by the kerb. 'He *does* live here. So far, so good!'

Mandy frowned. 'Who? ... Hey, isn't that Robbie Jones's bike?' She recognised the gleaming machine with a long scratch along the shiny petrol tank.

James nodded and took the steps to the white front door two at a time. He firmly pressed the bell next to a little plaque saying Flat C, and waited.

'Hi there.' A woman with red hair answered the door. She took in Mandy and James standing damp and breathless on the doorstep.

'We've come to see Robbie,' James explained.

'Hang on.' She turned and yelled casually along the hallway. 'Robbie, you've got visitors!' Then she wandered off into a side room.

Loud footsteps clumped down wooden stairs. Robbie Jones appeared in T-shirt, motorbike trousers and boots. 'Hi!' he said, recognising them from the end of the long hall. 'I wasn't expecting to see you.'

Mandy leaned against the doorpost to catch her breath. She heard James clear his throat as Robbie approached, running a hand through his hair and giving them a puzzled look.

'This might come as a surprise,' James began. 'But don't say "no" straight away. Stop and think about it.'

'Think about what?' Robbie rested one arm against the open door and waited.

'Adopting Rupert,' James said out of the blue. 'After all he's been through, don't you think you could give him a home?'

'But I don't know anything about dogs!' Robbie protested. It had taken him a few seconds to get his voice back after the surprise James had given him. The woman with the red hair had drifted back into the hallway.

'No, but you do like Rupert.' Mandy had gathered her wits. *Brilliant*! she thought, the moment James had popped the question. *Just like James to have thought of this!* 'You care about him, don't you?'

'Yeah.' Robbie had to admit that he did.

'And he likes you,' she insisted. 'You can tell

he does by the way he wags his tail when you visit him.'

'He never bore me a grudge for knocking him down,' Robbie agreed. 'Which is amazing, really.'

'Which dog are you talking about?' the woman wanted to know. Her freckled, pretty face looked concerned. 'My name's Jan. I'm Robbie's girlfriend,' she explained.

Jan's long red hair and slim figure reminded Mandy of her own mother. She wished Emily were here now to help convince Jan and Robbie to adopt Rupert.

'The little mongrel,' James told her. 'He's got over his dislocated hip, but he's homeless.'

'Poor thing.' Jan considered Rupert's predicament. She glanced at Robbie with troubled, greeny-grey eyes.

'Whoa!' Robbie backed off under the pressure. 'It's one thing visiting the dog a couple of times to see how he is. But this is serious commitment you're talking about here.'

'That's right,' Mandy agreed. There'd be no point going on with this if Robbie wasn't one hundred per cent sure.

James too fell silent. He took off his glasses and wiped them on his sweatshirt. His shoulders slumped and he stared at his feet.

'Where's this dog now?' Jan broke the awkward silence.

'Still at the hospital,' Mandy murmured. She looked from Jan to Robbie, then at James's disappointed, downcast face.

The young woman touched Robbie's elbow lightly with her fingertips. 'Why don't we go down and take another look at him?' she suggested quietly. 'Where would be the harm in that?'

Mandy heard James take a deep breath. She saw him look at his watch.

'You'll have to be quick!' James said, fixing his glasses firmly on his nose. 'It's nearly eleven. At twelve o'clock they plan to send Rupert away!'

Ten

'Why didn't you tell me what was going on?' Mandy demanded.

She and James stood by the entrance to the Tube station, waiting for Danny Davies to show up so that they could all drive on to Fitzroy Court. They'd already watched Robbie Jones and his girlfriend set off on the bike for the animal hospital, and now Mandy wanted to know why James hadn't let her in on his secret plan.

'Because it might not have worked out,' he told her, looking anxiously up and down the street for Danny's white van. 'Like I said, it was a long shot, and I didn't want to get your hopes up too high.'

'It still might not work out,' she reminded him. Robbie had insisted that adopting Rupert would be a big move. He was only going along to the hospital to take another look; no promises, no decisions.

James held up his hand with fingers crossed. 'Let's hope. Anyway, what's happened to Danny?'

Mandy saw a silver car draw up by the kerb and recognised the inspector as he leaned across the passenger's side to beckon them. 'Here he is.' She ran to the car and opened the door. 'Where's your van?' she asked as she slid in, noticing Bandit sitting quietly in the back.

'At the hospital,' Danny told her. 'The RSPCA van makes us too obvious. We don't get police support on a first attempt to serve a summons, so we needed an unmarked car so as not to give Carl Hickmann a chance to spot us and run off.'

James climbed into the back seat. 'Move over, Bandit!'

The bull terrier shifted his bulky frame. He settled again at James's feet, his thin tail wagging gently.

'What's Bandit doing here?' Mandy asked as the car pulled out into the road.

'I promised Mrs Powers I'd take him on a first visit to see his prospective new owners when we've finished at Fitzroy Court. They live in the same part of town.'

James and Mandy were glad to have the terrier's company. He took their minds off any problems they might have when they came to serve the summons on Carl Hickmann.

'He weighs a ton!' James complained, as they wove their way through heavy traffic. 'Bandit, did you know you were lying on my feet?'

'Let him come in the front where there's more room,' Mandy suggested. She looked round and smiled at the terrier as he blinked and yawned. He opened his enormous mouth and showed her his sharp, vicious-looking teeth.

'It's not worth it. We're nearly there.' Danny pointed to Fitzroy Court, just ahead. They approached on the inside lane, signalled and came off the carriageway into the parking spaces at the foot of the building.

Danny coasted along between the parked cars and vans. 'I want to find a spot that gives us a good view of the second floor,' he explained.

'We should sit here for a bit, rather than rush straight up.'

Mandy stared out of the window. The block of flats towered over them, backed by a grey, drizzling sky. She felt her mouth go dry and her heartbeat quicken at the thought of what they were about to do.

'It doesn't look like there's anyone around.' James disturbed Bandit to move his feet and slide across the back seat for a better view. 'I can see Lisa's flat from here. The door's shut.'

At last Danny found a good place to park. He put on the handbrake and wound down the window. 'We wait,' he said again. 'I don't want to rush this.'

Mandy agreed. They needed to work things out in case Hickmann made a run for it. 'The lift is about fifty metres along the landing to the right of the flat,' she pointed out, leaning out of her window. 'Is that the only way in and out?'

'It's the only one I've noticed.' Danny scanned the building. 'But there must be a back way we don't know about. Every block of flats has stairs as well as a lift.'

'Hang on!' James had kept his eyes on the door of number 28. 'The door's opening. Someone's coming out!'

Mandy and Danny pulled themselves quickly back inside the car. They watched two figures leave the flat and close the door behind them.

'One's Lisa!' James recognised the small, dark-haired woman.

'The other one must be Anne-Marie!' Mandy noticed the same slight figure, though the second woman had longer hair and looked younger. They walked along the balcony towards the lift, pressed the button and waited for it to arrive.

'Make sure they don't see us!' Danny warned, hunching down in his seat.

'It's OK, they've gone the other way.' Mandy saw the lift arrive at the ground floor and watched Lisa and Anne-Marie walk off, chatting casually. 'Do you think Hickmann is still in the flat?'

'I don't know, but it could be time to find out.' Danny waited for the women to disappear from view, checked that he had the summons safe in his shirt pocket, then opened the car door. 'You two wait here with Bandit,' he ordered.

'Why?' James was disappointed to be left behind. He held on tight to the terrier's collar. Bandit had raised his front paws on to the back seat to look out of the window.

'Can't we come?' Mandy asked.

'No. It's safer if I go up by myself. Three of us going to the door are more likely to scare him off than just one.' Danny looked nervous as he glanced up at the second floor. 'Wish me luck,' he said as he set off.

'Let's hope Hickmann's in,' James whispered.

Mandy watched Danny head across the car park to the main entrance. A woman with a German shepherd on a lead wheeled a pushchair past him as he entered the lift.

Bandit saw the dog and barked. The German shepherd snarled and barked back.

'Shh!' Mandy warned. All the doors on the second floor stayed tight shut. But she saw the net curtains of Number 28 move to one side. 'Hickmann must be in!' she hissed.

'Has he seen us?' James hung on to Bandit. The other dog was straining at the lead and still barking as the woman struggled to control him. Eventually she managed to drag the German shepherd into a ground-floor flat.

'I don't think so.' Mandy shrank back into the car. 'But he heard the dogs making a row. Danny's on his way up, and Hickmann's still at the window!' The net curtains were open, and now she could see a face peering through the glass. 'Danny's there! He's stepping out on to the balcony. Hickmann's seen him!'

Suddenly the net curtain dropped into place and the face disappeared. As Danny set off from the lift along the balcony, the door to Number 28 was flung open. The inspector stopped in his tracks.

Carl Hickmann rushed out of the flat carrying the first thing he'd been able to grab. It was a metal kitchen chair, which he swung over his head as he charged at Danny.

'Come on!' Mandy saw what was happening and leaped from the car. No way could they sit and watch Hickmann attack Danny.

Up on the balcony, Hickmann swung the chair and brought it crashing down on the inspector. Danny put up his arms to defend himself, but he went down, out of sight. His attacker flung the chair on top of him, turned and ran back along the balcony.

'James, let Bandit out of the car!' Mandy yelled. She wrenched open the back door, turned and saw Hickmann reach the end of the balcony, swing round the corner and vanish. 'Get him!' she cried to the bull terrier. 'Go on, Bandit; fetch!'

The terrier lowered his massive head and charged for the far side of the building. His powerful body pounded across the carpark. With their hearts in their mouths, Mandy and James followed.

They heard footsteps running and sliding down hidden stairs. They rounded the corner and saw a flight of concrete steps. Then Hickmann appeared, sweating and out of breath, just as Bandit reached the bottom of the stairwell.

The bull terrier reared up. He snarled at Hickmann and drove him into a corner.

'Help! Get him off me!' the terrified, drunken man cried as he tripped and fell.

Bandit cornered him. He stood over Hickmann, lips curled back, showing two rows of ferocious teeth.

Mandy heard more footsteps coming downstairs. 'Good boy, Bandit! Keep him there until Danny arrives!'

The sturdy dog stood his ground over the trembling man.

'It's OK, Danny. Bandit's got him cornered!' James yelled up the stairs.

At last the inspector arrived. There was a cut on his cheek, he was winded by the blow from the chair. But he pulled a white envelope out of his pocket and thrust it under Hickmann's sweating face. 'You're not getting away with it this time!' he gasped. 'Carl Hickmann, I'm an inspector from the RSPCA and this is an order for you to appear in court on a charge of cruelty to animals!'

'What happened to you?' Wendy Davies ran to meet Danny as he came through the main doors of the animal hospital. She'd got a cab over there as soon as Barney had called with the message that Danny had been hurt.

The inspector put a hand to his bloody cheek. He felt all eyes in the busy waiting-room on him and blushed. 'Nothing. Don't worry. It's only a scratch.'

'We did it. We served the summons!' Mandy followed Danny through the door. Behind her, James was letting Bandit out of the car.

Bandit trotted up the ramp and trundled through the door, head up, proud of his morning's work.

'Take him to the kennels,' Barney told James and Mandy, steering Bandit away from the dogs in the waiting area. 'Give him a good drink and settle him down. His visit to his prospective owners will have to be rescheduled. He's had enough excitement for one day!'

'Well done.' Sara Exley came out of a treatment room to congratulate them. 'I heard about Carl Hickmann. Now you can be sure that justice will be done!'

Mandy nodded and smiled. 'This feels good!' she whispered to James as they took Bandit through the door into the kennels.

'And this is going to feel even better!' James stopped her from going forward. 'Look!'

There in the kennels were Robbie Jones and his girlfriend, Jan. They were with Julie Ashe, who was giving them forms to sign and explaining exactly how the couple could adopt a dog from the RSPCA.

'Danny said he didn't have any problem getting Hickmann to sign Rupert over to us. He explained to Hickmann that his punishment might be less harsh if he admitted cruelty,' Julie told them. 'But in any case, the court would never send Rupert back to live with him again. And he might well be prosecuted for attacking Danny, as well as being fined and banned from keeping pets!' Julie added.

'So he can come and live with us?' Jan smiled

down at the small cream mongrel. She bent and picked him up.

'Soon,' Julie agreed.

Robbie put his arm round Jan's shoulder and stroked their new pet. Rupert wriggled and licked his hand. His brown eyes gleamed from behind his shaggy fringe. 'How soon?' Robbie asked.

'Let's say Friday,' the nurse told them. 'Come back then when all the forms have been signed, and you can take Rupert home.'

'. . . And then Hickmann attacked Danny with a chair, but Bandit saved him. He got Hickmann in a corner and scared him while Danny served the summons!' Mandy had gone up to intensive care to tell Sasha about their success.

The beagle raised her head. Her soft brown ears fell back from her face to show an alert, clear gaze. She seemed to take in every word.

'James is really happy because Robbie Jones has adopted Rupert,' Mandy told Sasha. 'It was James's idea. Brilliant, wasn't it?'

Sasha wagged her tail.

'Of course, I'm happy too. But I'm still a bit worried about you.' Mandy stood over the unit, knowing how much work the vets and nurses had put in to pull the beagle through this far. She knew too that, until Sasha was eating and drinking for herself, they still had a fight on their hands.

Mandy thought for a moment, then went on. 'Maybe I shouldn't mention this, but Wendy still isn't sleeping very well and Danny finds it hard sometimes to keep his mind on his job.' She sighed and spoke quietly. 'What we all need is for you to show us that you really are getting better!'

Sasha tilted her head to follow Mandy as she walked slowly round the unit. The scar on her head was beginning to heal, her breathing was deep and even.

'Barney says you might not get your strength back for a long time because of what you've been through. But James and I go home on Friday. Wouldn't it be great if you could stand up by yourself before then?'

The dog listened and followed Mandy's movements. She seemed to make a decision and gather her strength. Slowly she folded her front legs underneath her body and pushed herself up.

Mandy saw her trying to sit up and gasped. 'Oh, you good girl!'

Sasha's front legs wobbled and almost gave way. Her head dipped towards the blanket, then lifted again. Once more, she pushed.

'That's it. You're sitting!' Mandy coaxed the dog up. For the first time since the accident Sasha was willing herself to move. Mandy eased in close and ran the flat of her hand down the dog's smooth white chest. 'You're a brave, brave dog!' she murmured. Her voice croaked, then broke down.

Sasha nudged Mandy's hand with her soft nose, as if telling her there was no need to worry.

Mandy gazed into the dog's constant, loving eyes.

'OK, I won't worry any more,' she told her, wiping her wet cheeks. Now she truly believed that Sasha would get well. She smiled through her tears. 'This must seem strange to you, but it's what people do. I'm not crying because I'm sad but because I'm really, really happy!'

If you enjoyed this Animal Ark Story, look out for the Animal Ark Christmas Special, *Hamster in the Holly* – here's an extract to whet your appetite!

'Er, Mandy . . .' James cut in as Mandy practised her witch's cackle for the school play for the fourth time. He was standing at the door of the lab with small, fair-haired Daniel Winterton, the music teacher's seven-year-old son. 'I told Daniel he could come and look at Henry.'

Mandy went on with her lines. ' "You've come just in the nick of time! After tomorrow's sunrise, I could do nothing to help you for another year!" ' She laughed again, plucking imaginary toads from her hair and shoulders.

Daniel pulled a scared face and backed away.

'It's OK,' James coaxed. 'Take no notice of Mandy. Come and see the hamster.'

The younger boy sidled into the room after James and crept up to Henry's cage. The class pet trundled gamely on inside his wheel.

'Daniel was bored,' James explained. 'He's had to sit through weeks of rehearsals while his mum's been busy with the play. And it just so happens he likes hamsters, don't you, Daniel?'

'I love them.' His pale, round face had broken into a smile as he watched Henry turn the wheel. 'I had one when I was four years old. I called him Norvik. He liked to climb up the curtains. He was a satin-coated Himalayan hamster with red eyes.' The smile faded as he spoke.

'What happened to him?' Mandy asked.

'He died.' Daniel sighed. 'We found him covered in a pile of wood shavings in the corner of his cage. He probably felt poorly while we were at school and crept in there. When we got home, he was dead.'

'I'm sorry,' Mandy said quietly, gazing over Daniel's shoulder at sturdy, lively Henry and feeling glad that he was healthy. She knew that small pets like hamsters could go downhill very quickly once they grew ill. 'Maybe you can get another hamster soon.'

Quickly Daniel Winterton shook his head. 'Mum doesn't like hamsters or mice, and because Dad isn't around much to help any more, she says I'll have to wait until I'm older and able to look after it myself. Anyway, it wouldn't be the same. Norvik was special.'

As his voice trailed off, Henry stopped trundling and hopped out of his wheel. He came to the front of his cage in short, nervous bursts, then poked his little pink nose through the bars.

'He's saying hello.' Mandy felt sorry for the sad little boy. She'd noticed him in the assembly hall where they rehearsed the Christmas play, hidden away in a corner, reading or writing in a notebook he always carried with him. He looked lonely, but Mrs Winterton seemed too busy to notice.

'Hello,' Daniel whispered to Henry, reaching out gently to touch the hamster's nose.

'Daniel! There you are!' Mrs Winterton bustled into the lab. She was obviously taking a well-earned break from rehearsals and had come looking for her son. She was a thin, pretty woman with thick, jet-black hair and big brown eyes, not at all like Daniel. Today she was dressed for action in a long, pale blue shirt and black leggings.

'I might have known this was where you'd be!' she exclaimed, noticing Henry in his cage. 'Hamsters!' She raised her finely arched eyebrows at Mandy and James. 'I can't keep him away.'

'Look, Mum, he's saying hello.' Daniel pointed to Henry, who was still grabbing the cage wire with his front paws and poking his nose through the gaps.

'Come on, Daniel, I haven't time to look. I've a million things to do,' Mrs Winterton said. 'I want you back in the hall where I can keep an eye on you. And Mandy and James, could you go to the art room for costume fittings with Miss Temple? You have five minutes before we start on Act Two, so please get a move on.'

' 'Bye, Henry!' Daniel gave the hamster one last stroke.

'You can see him again soon,' his mother promised, waiting impatiently by the door. She marched her son down the corridor to the hall.

'Be good, Henry,' James joked, tickling his stomach through the wire mesh.

The hamster seemed to sigh as he dropped to the floor of his cage and waddled away. Back to the exercise wheel: *squeak-squeak-squeak*.

Mandy took a long, last look, smiled, then turned off the light.

'That's good, Mandy!' Mrs Winterton was happy with her cackle at last.

Mandy held up her hands and wiggled her fingers in a scary, witchlike way. She drove the mermaids away with a fierce shriek.

'Very good!' From her seat at the piano, the music teacher praised Mandy's dramatic exit. 'Mermaids, you must hold the long notes. And more volume, please. Now, one more time!'

Her part finished for now, Mandy slipped from the stage and made her way across the hall. She was looking for Daniel, to ask him more about his hamster, Norvik.

'Have you seen Daniel Winterton?' she asked Susan Collins.

The star of the show was busy learning her lines at the back of the hall. 'Not lately,' she murmured, without looking up.

'Try the art room,' Vicky Simpson suggested. Vicky was packing away the violin that she played in the school orchestra and taking it along the corridor to the music department's store room. 'Miss Temple's still in there doing costumes. Maybe Daniel got bored and went along.'

'No, sorry, I haven't seen him.' Miss Temple said when Mandy went to ask. James was standing very still while the biology teacher stuck dressmakers' pins into his shirt. It was too big and needed to be taken in.

'Try the biology lab,' he suggested. 'You

know . . . hamster . . . Daniel . . . *Ouch*!' A needle had pricked his arm.

'Don't move!' Miss Temple ordered.

So Mandy backtracked down the corridor to the lab. The light was off, the room in darkness. Not here either, she said to herself. But something made her step inside the door.

It's too quiet! She listened for the squeak of Henry's wheel and heard only silence. *Perhaps he's asleep. No, hamsters come out at night. He should be moving about*. Worried thoughts flashed through her head as she crept across the darkened room, past the long benches where the classes did their practical biology work, towards the shelf where Henry's cage stood. The only light came from the street lamps in the road outside, which cast a strange orange glare.

'Henry?' Mandy leaned forward to examine the cage.

Nothing. No squeak of the wheel, no curious little brown and white face at the grille.

'Henry!' Gripped by real fear, Mandy reached out for the cage door. It swung open to her touch.

'Oh, no!' Swiftly she looked inside, amongst the piles of wood-shavings, under the plastic toy log in one corner, behind the exercise wheel, inside the small nest-box where the hamster slept. Empty!

Mandy backed off, looking wildly along the shelf. She fell to the floor and scrabbled between the benches and stools. Nothing.

Then she got up and ran for the assembly hall. She flew down the big room to the piano where the music teacher was playing. 'Please stop, Mrs Winterton!' she begged, her hair flying across her face, her arms waving in the direction from which she'd come.

'Mandy, whatever is the matter?' The teacher stood up. Everyone onstage stared at Mandy. Susan and Vicky came forward from the back of the hall. Daniel crept to his mother's side.

'Oh, quick!' she gasped. 'I need some help. Henry's escaped from his cage. We have to find him!'

ANIMAL ACTION

If you like *Animal Ark* then you'll love the RSPCA's Animal Action Club! Anyone aged 13 or under can become a member for just £5.50 a year. Join up and you can look forward to six issues of Animal Action magazine - each one is bursting with animal news, competitions, features, posters and celebrity interviews. Plus we'll send you a fantastic joining pack too!

To be really animal-friendly just complete the form – a photocopy is fine – and send it, with a cheque or postal order for £5.50  (made payable to the RSPCA), to Animal Action Club, RSPCA, Causeway, Horsham, West Sussex RH12 1HG. We'll then send you a joining pack and your first copy of *Animal Action*.

Registered charity no 219099

Don't delay, join today!

Name

....

Address

....

....

Postcode

....

Date of birth

....

Youth membership of the Royal Society for the Prevention of Cruelty to Animals

AACHOD2